The Other Side:
Secrets

By O'Jay Barr

Above the
BARR PUBLISHING

Copyright © 2021, O'Jay Barr

Cover image: © 2021

ISBN: 13:978-1-7372584-2-1

Publisher's Note

Printed and bound in the United States of America. All rights reserved. No part of this book may be reproduced or transmitted in any form or by any means, electronic or mechanical, including photocopying, recording, or by any information storage and retrieval system except by a review who may quote brief passages in a review to be printed in a magazine, newspaper, or on the Web without permission in writing from **O'Jay Barr**.

Although the author and publisher have made every effort to ensure the accuracy and completeness of information contained in this book, we assume no responsibility for errors, inaccuracies, omissions, or any inconsistency herein. Neither the publisher nor the author shall be liable for damages arising from here.

DEDICATION

I dedicate this book to anyone who has ever doubted themselves, as a reminder that anything is possible. Thank you to everyone who has ever believed in me. To my circle, those that read all my edits, provided feedback or even just an encouraging word - thank you.

A special thank you to my wonderful wife and daughters. I couldn't have done this without the love and support that you show me every day. I love you more than words.

SAMANTHA

"Hey, boss lady. These flowers were just delivered for you. Aren't they beautiful?! You want them in the usual spot?"

I gasped as I looked up from my computer to see the bouquet my assistant, Erica, was carrying.

"Yes, that's fine," I answered, trying not to seem as flustered as I felt.

"I need me somebody like Darrin. I mean you two have been together for years and he still sends you flowers every other week like clockwork. I don't think I've ever seen roses like these. What are they called?" Erica rambled on as she walked across to the huge picture window overlooking the Atlanta Skyline.

"On second thought don't put them there! Put them on the bookcase in the corner," I all but yelled.

"In the corner? No one will be able to see them over there. This is where you always put them so people can see them when they pass by." Erica already had the rainbow roses on the table in front of the window and was adjusting the arrangement so that the best side was facing out.

"Erica put the flowers where I told you and get back to work. We don't have time to be distracted by silly roses when we have a deadline for this huge account in two days." I snapped while pretending to be immersed into my computer. I watched out of the corner of my eye as Erica rolled her eyes while moving the roses over to the bookcase and strutted out of my office, closing the door behind her.

As soon as Erica closed the door, I pushed my chair back from my desk and stared at the roses.

Why would Darrin send me rainbow roses? Does he know that I am gay? Well can I be gay if I haven't had sex with a woman...yet...I mean before? Do my extremely vivid wet dreams count? Ugh what is going on with me! Maybe I should talk to Josephine. She's not going to take me seriously but I gotta do something. I picked up my cell phone and called my sister before I talked myself out of it.

She answered on the first ring, "Wassup?"

"Hey twin! Want to meet for lunch today? My treat!"

"What's wrong?"

"Huh? Why does something have to be wrong for me to want to take you to lunch?"

"Because it usually is," Josephine chuckled.

"Never mind Josephine. I just wanted to spend time with my sister but since you..."

"Okay Sam chill out. I'll meet you at noon at the diner downtown. Is that cool or would you prefer something more high class?"

"The diner is fine Jo." I hung up quickly before I got more agitated or she changed her mind.

I arrived at the diner a few minutes early to mentally prepare myself to talk to my twin about my sexuality questions. I would never admit it to her but I valued her opinion more than anybody else. She was low key my hero. At 29 she was an officer in the Air Force, she's been openly gay since high school and in short she's just badass. I smiled to myself remembering how she came out to our parents in 9th grade. She announced it about 15 minutes before her girlfriend came over for dinner one night. I thought I was going to have a heart attack but not Jo, she said it so nonchalantly that I don't even think my parents reacted.

I snapped out of my trip down memory lane at the sound of a motorcycle outside. A couple of seconds later my beautiful sister strolled in, she flashed her smile when she saw me sitting in our favorite booth in the back. I couldn't help but notice how both men and women turned to watch her as she walked through the restaurant. I mean who could blame them. Jo was a couple inches taller than me at 5'9" about 160 pounds, caramel skin covered in tattoos, we both had curly hair but she wore her curls in a cute short cut while most of the time I wore my hair long and straight. She was wearing jean shorts with a tank top and boots. While her outfit complimented her curvy figure it was her perfect smile and confidence that usually turned heads. Just seeing her instantly calmed me down. Call it twin powers or some B.S. When Jo reached the booth she kissed me on the cheek before sitting down across from me.

"Hey twin, you look nice today." Jo said as she put her helmet on the seat next to her.

"You don't look so shabby yourself twin. Well at least that's what half the people in here think." I giggled because as usual Jo was oblivious to anyone trying to catch her eye. My twin knew she was attractive, she was just short of being conceited but unless you were on her radar she could care less.

"I have no idea what you're talking about. Did you order me…"

"A sweet tea with extra lemon and an order of cheese fries. Yeah it should be out in a minute."

"Thanks. So what's been up?"

"I think we should have a 30th birthday party together," I saw my twin tilt her head and squint, so before she could question if that was the real reason for our impromptu lunch date, I jumped right into the proposal that I was making up as I went along, "We could have it at one of your clubs and invite everybody. Come on sis we haven't had a party together since…."

"Since our 18th, when I beat up your boyfriend for making out with my girlfriend."

"You mean when I beat up your girlfriend for making out with my boyfriend."

We both laughed. That night was crazy and the longest my twin and I went without talking- 2 weeks- until our sister Charlotte got us together to remind us we were both stupid and stubborn.

"Damn we've grown so much since then." We both said in unison and then laughed again.

"I think a party together would be dope Sam. Let's do it!"

The waitress arrived with our food so we paused long enough to dig in. I took the opportunity to switch gears and get into the real reason we were there, even though I really was excited about the party idea.

"Jo when did you realize you liked girls?"

Jo paused, with cheese fry in mid air to think for a minute. She smiled, stuck the fry in her mouth and answered, "in 1st grade when you were friends with Carmen. She was my first love."

I burst out laughing as my sister closed her eyes reminiscing about Carmen.

"I'm serious Jo," I said while still laughing.

"Shit me too! Carmen was my first crush. One day I tried to kiss her on the cheek and she ran away yelling Josephine likes girls, Josephine likes girls. She broke my heart," Jo said while pretending to wipe away imaginary tears. She saw me rolling my eyes and said "ok, ok seriously it was the summer between seventh and eighth grade. Remember that was the first summer mom and dad let us go to separate summer camps? I was so nervous yet excited to be on my own. It was different being apart but I felt like…and don't take this the wrong way…that for the first time I could explore my own identity and not just be one of the twins."

"I know exactly what you mean. I felt the same way and then I felt bad for feeling that way."

"Me too! But I always felt that it made us closer. You know the 'saying absence'....."

"Makes the heart grow fonder" I smiled as I finished my sister's sentence, "anyway, please finish."

"Okay so the junior counselor assigned to my cabin was only a few years older than me, I think she was 15. The first couple of nights there I had a hard time sleeping so I would sit up with her and talk. We legit talked about everything. She was gay and she would tell me about her girlfriends and when she realized she liked girls. I think she sensed it in me before I did because now that I think about it the conversation was kind of random. Anyway, one night she asked me if I wanted to kiss her. I kind of freaked out, thanks to Carmen, and said no.

She didn't get mad or anything she just smiled and said okay. The next night, I asked her if her offer to kiss her was still on the table and the rest I guess you could say is history." Jo shrugged nonchalantly, just like she did when she announced the news to our parents all those years ago.

"Whoa, so Jo you had sex with her?!" I exclaimed, a little shocked.

"Jeez, Sam keep your voice down. No I did not have sex with her. We kissed…..a lot. She was a great kisser might I add. We made out a couple times but that was it. I didn't sleep with her until the next summer," Jo added laughing as she saw my face.

"Oh…."

"Why the sudden questions about my lesbian curiosity? You've never asked me about any of this before," Jo asked, drinking her tea and squinting her eyes suspiciously at me.

"No reason. I just realized you never told me about it. Kind of like you woke up one day and decided to be gay."

"I didn't **decide** to be gay Sam," Jo said a little rougher than I expected, "I always felt different. I just didn't know what was wrong with me. It wasn't until Valerie and that summer alone that I was able to fully explore me and to be confident in being me. She helped me realize there was nothing wrong with me."

"I'm sorry I didn't mean to offend you. I guess I'm just trying to understand that's all. I…. never mind," I started but couldn't figure out the right words, sipping my tea to fight back tears.

"It's okay, Sam, you didn't offend me. I know you mean well. I appreciate you wanting to understand."

As Jo was talking a single tear escaped out of the corner of my left eye and down my cheek before

I could wipe it away. Jo reached across the table and covered my hand with hers to comfort me.

The waitress appeared at the most inconvenient time to check in. Without looking up, Jo ordered a white wine spritzer and another sweet tea.

As soon as the waitress walked away Jo asked, "Is something else going on Samantha? Why are you crying?"

The waitress returned and placed the drinks on the table. I took a sip of the wine spritzer and collected my thoughts before answering my twin.

"I've been having these dreams lately," I started.

"Okay, what kind of dreams?" Jo interrupted.

"Wet dreams?"

"Ohhkaaay……"

"About women." I blurted out before I could lose my nerve.

"OH! Ohhhh…" Jo said as her brain registered what I said. She reached across the table, picked up my wine spritzer and downed the rest of the glass in one gulp.

Seeing my usually put together twin so flustered made me giggle.

Jo rolled her eyes at me and raised the glass in the air signaling to the waitress to bring another. I giggled more.

"Are you okay Jo?" I managed to get out between giggles.

"I'm good. So about these dreams… is it someone you know? When did they start? Have you acted on them?" Jo rambled off questions as the waitress came to the table with another wine spritzer.

"No, a couple of months ago and no. But I think I want to." I answered each question as I finally stopped laughing at my twin.

"Oh...."

"Can you please say something besides 'oh' Josie?" I reverted to my childhood nickname for her and reached for her wine spritzer. She slapped my hand away and picked the glass up. "Hey! You drank mine so technically...."

"Yeah, yeah," Jo cut me off and took a sip before handing the glass to me, "back to the matter at hand. You definitely caught me off guard Sam. I wasn't expecting that. Does Darrin know? Okay, forget I asked," Jo saw the panic in my eyes at that last question. "This doesn't necessarily mean anything Samantha. You're probably freaking yourself out for nothing. Dreams don't mean....."

I cut her off, "But Jo I WANT to. The last several months, things with Darrin haven't been the same. At first I thought maybe the spark was gone so I tried to spice things up a little. We started regular date nights and I bought all this stuff for the bedroom. I know TMI but bare with me. I quickly realized it didn't matter what we used in the bedroom, I just didn't want to use it with him. When he touches me I practically cringe inside. I would have described our sex life before as average but now... I don't know. The feeling I have with Darrin is nothing compared to my dreams. I've never experienced anything like this before and I am yearning to have it for real. I've just been feeling….."

"Different?" Jo offered quietly.

"Yeah ...different. Don't get me wrong Darrin is amazing and I love him. I thought I wanted to spend the rest of my life with him but I need to make sure. Maybe I'm making more out of this then necessary. Sex isn't everything right? I'm so confused Josie," my eyes welled up with tears.

"Please don't cry Sam. If you cry then I'm going to cry and you know I don't cry. We'll figure this out...together. I promise. Okay?" Jo reached across the table again and squeezed my hand. I nodded and finished off the wine spritzer. I smiled at my twin and felt relieved that I talked to her. I still had no idea what I was going to do but the fact that I finally shared my secret was a huge load off.

I strolled into my office after lunch feeling like a totally different person. Once at my desk, I called Erica to come into my office for our afternoon meeting. She came in with her iPad and I could tell she was still a little upset from this morning. She sat on the other side of my desk and started with her updates. As she was talking I slid a small bag from the diner across the desk to her. She pushed the bag back and said "no thank you. I ate lunch at my desk while working on the Harris proposal."

"Oh okay well I'm stuffed but I guess I could make room for turtle chee.."

"On second thought, I can always go for cheesecake," Erica blurted as she grabbed the bag off the desk and opened it while laughing.

I giggled as she moaned with her eyes closed after putting the first forkful in her mouth.

"I just wanted to apologize for snapping on you this morning. It's been a long week but I shouldn't have taken it out on you. I was thinking about going out for drinks tonight. Want to come? Maybe I'll see if Josephine wants to come too!" I said excitedly.

"First cheesecake and then the promise of drinks with your sexy ass sister. You must really be sorry!" Erica laughed in between bites of cheesecake.

I laughed remembering that Erica had a crush on my twin. "Erica why do you always joke about liking Jo when you know you claim to be strictly dickly?"

"Because I am positive that your sister could turn me out honey and I am more than willing to let her try! Those lips, and arms, and tattoos oh and her….."

"Okay, okay I get it! I do not need to hear all that. She is still my sister," I laughed while putting my fingers in my ears like a little kid.

"My bad. I get carried away thinking about all that caramel goodness," Erica licked actual caramel off the fork with a faraway look in her eyes.

"Anyway…." I rolled my eyes, "I will text her to see if she has plans. If we can get the proposal finished in the next hour then we can leave for the day. Want to stay at my place? We can have a whole girls weekend with mimosas and massages tomorrow!"

"Hell yeah. Benefits of being best friends with the boss! But isn't it you and Darrin's date weekend?"

"He's working this weekend," I quickly lied and made a mental note to text him to cancel our plans as soon as I got a second, "so where are we with the Harris proposal?" I quickly changed the subject.

"It's done. I made all the changes after the last draft and added what we talked about at yesterday's meeting." Erica slid the iPad to me with the proposal already open. I read it while she finished off the last of the cheesecake. I could see her scraping the container and licking the fork out of the corner of my eye.

"It's gone Erica," I said without looking up from the iPad. I could also see her roll her eyes while still licking the fork before she put it and the empty container back in the bag.

"Wow Erica! This is really good. You really got everything from the concept meeting yesterday and some things that I even missed! With this proposal we are definitely a shoe in for this account. We'll send it off Monday morning but for now let's get out of here and pre-celebrate!"

"Thanks Samantha! I appreciate the support and you letting me handle the proposal pretty much by myself. I can be ready in 15 minutes. I want to check my emails and voicemails before we leave." Erica got up from my desk grabbing the iPad and the bag with her.

"Okay cool. Make it quick" I yelled after her as she walked out and I picked up my cell phone.

First, let me shoot Darrin a text canceling our plans and then to Jo to convince her to come hang out.

```
Sam: Hey baby.  Thank you so much
for the beautiful roses!  They were
very  eye-catching.    I  hope  you
don't mind but I want to reschedule
```

> our date weekend to next weekend. It's been a rough week here at the office so me and Erica are going to have a little girl's time. I promise to make it up to you next week.
>
> *Sam: Hey Josie! Thanks again for everything at lunch today. Want to go out for drinks tonight?*
>
> Erica's coming too.
>
> Josephine: I'll be at your place by 10:30.

Jo responded in record time. I knew that second text would do the trick. I smiled as I grabbed my purse and phone and got up from my desk. As I walked to the door, I got a text notification from Darrin.

> Hey my love. I'm glad you liked the roses. All proceeds from the sales go to a shelter for LGBT homeless youth. Enjoy your weekend with Erica baby. I have some work I need to catch up on anyway. See you Sunday for dinner? I love you.
>
> Oh that's awesome about the shelter! I love you too baby. See you Sunday.

I started feeling emotional and guilty about my negative thoughts toward Darrin. I knew I loved him but I was just so confused. Luckily, Erica popped her head in the door at the perfect moment, "you ready to go boss lady?"

"Yes! Let's go boo!" I linked my arm through hers and we strutted to the elevator.

JOSEPHINE

"Samantha! Someone's at the door!" I could hear Erica yell through Sam's condo.

"It's Jo! I'll be down in a minute!" Samantha yelled back.

Next, I heard Erica's heels clicking towards the door while she mumbled something about 'sexy'. I leaned against the door frame and when she opened the door I flashed my killer smile, "hey beautiful." Erica looked good as always. She had on a pair of jeans that were painted on her petite frame and a low-cut midriff-baring top. Even her feet were cute in the open-toed heels she was wearing.

"Hey, Jo." Erica smiled seductively at me and stepped back to let me in. She closed the door and turned around and I let out a low whistle. "Can I get a hug though?" I moved in before she could respond, knowing she wouldn't say no. I bent down and wrapped my arms around her waist and she whispered: "Damn you smell good." Her body all but melted into mine but then behind us, I heard, "Ahem! Josephine, please get your hands off my best friend's ass!"

I backed up and turned around smiling with my hands held out innocently. "These hands? Come on sis you know me better than that." I chuckled, kissed her on the cheek and headed to the kitchen to make a drink. They both followed me in the kitchen and I couldn't help but notice Erica was more than a little red. I winked at her when she finally looked my way. She smiled into her glass and Sam rolled her eyes. "I wish you two would just sleep with each other already and get it over with! The sexual tension between you is intense and annoying! Make me a drink too."

"I have no idea what you are talking about. Erica and I are just friends besides I don't do straight girls." I handed a glass to my sister and immediately noticed a shift in Erica's mood. Was this girl really feeling me? Cause I damn sure wanted a taste. I would have to talk to Sam to see if she would be okay before I made a move. She was her best friend and they worked together. If things went left it could be bad for their relationship. I must have been deep in thought because I looked up and saw both Erica and Sam staring at me like they were waiting for something.

"Huh?"

"Where are we going?" Sam asked impatiently.

"Why are you asking me? Didn't you invite me to hang out with you?" I leaned back against the marble countertop while sipping my drink.

"I know but I was hoping you could take us to one of your spots….." Sam gestured awkwardly with her hands and looked away.

"Oh...ohhhh! Okay..."

"Don't start that again Jo."

"Look, Jo are you gonna take us to a gay club or not?" Erica spoke for the first time since she greeted me at the door. She threw back a shot and looked at my twin and I. We were both staring at her a little shocked.

"Umm...."

"Look, your sister is curious as hell and I'm currently experiencing a drought so anywhere I can shake my ass and get some attention is good with me so let's go. Who's driving? I call shotgun!" And with that, she grabbed her purse and sauntered out the kitchen while I stared at her ass. Sam slapped me on the arm disturbing the explicit thoughts running through my head.

"Stop mentally undressing her and let's go. Oh, and you're driving cause I plan on getting fucked up tonight." Samantha ran after Erica leaving me standing in the kitchen trying to figure out what the hell just happened. I caught up to them at the elevator and put my arms around their shoulders.

"We can meet up with some of my crew at Graphic but don't say I didn't warn you. Oh and we all come back here TOGETHER!" I emphasized the last word.

"So you not leaving with some chick?" Erica said with a hint of jealousy in her voice.

"Yeah....you." I kissed her cheek and exited the elevator.

I didn't have to turn around to know my sister was rolling her eyes and Erica was blushing. I hit the alarm on my blue Mercedes truck and opened the passenger door for Erica. After closing her door, I opened the back door for my twin who was impatiently waiting her turn, I bowed slightly at the waist and motioned to the back seat. She giggled and slid in.

"Seat belts ladies. It's going to be a bumpy ride." Cruising the HOV lane we got to the club in no time. I pulled up to the front and tossed the keys to the valet. "Hey, Rodrick park her...."

"In the front. I know Jo. Tre and Bran are already here." The attendant handed me a ticket. I walked around the truck, where Erica and Sam were getting out of their already opened doors. We walked up to the VIP line, as we approached the new bouncer opened the door, "What's up Jo? Is this your....sister?" She asked too enthusiastically.

"Yes, this is my little sister Samantha," I responded protectively.

"Please, she's only 4 minutes older than me. This is Erica." Sam was smiling too bright as the bouncer looked her up and down like she was lunch. I motioned for them to walk ahead of me. I put my hand at the small of Erica's back as I followed close behind and side-eyed the bouncer that was about to be fired. Once we entered the club, I took the lead across the dance floor to our section where my two closest friends and business partners were already waiting. I dapped them both and then introduced Erica since they already knew Sam. Everyone sat down and started head bobbing to the music blasting from the speakers. I leaned over and whispered in Erica's ear asking what she wanted to drink. She smiled and turned so she could whisper back, "I can get my own drink...thanks." With that, she got up, grabbed my sister's hand and stepped out of the section. She glanced back over her shoulder once they were halfway to the bar to see if I was watching her walk away and I damn sure was. I finally tore my eyes off of her to see my boi's trying not to laugh.

"What?"

"Shiiiit you hitting that?" Tre asked.

"No, I told you that's Sam's best friend. I'm just being polite." I responded as my eyes searched the crowd at the bar until I spotted them. Sam had her arms across her chest and was talking to some chick. I started to get up and then I realized it was my ex- Monica. "Fuck" I muttered louder than I intended.

"Polite my ass....or should I say her ass?" Tre said while laughing.

"Is that Monica talking to Sam?" Bran asked squinting.

"Yeah. Man, I don't feel like dealing with her ass tonight. She finally stopped calling me a couple of weeks ago." I watched as Monica walked away from the bar and Sam headed to the dance floor. I couldn't find Erica but then I realized she was already on the dance floor grinding on some bitch. Normally, I would get up to mark my territory but one I realized she wasn't mine to mark...yet and two Erica was facing this way and staring directly at me. She was putting on a show. I sat back in my seat and relaxed while watching her perform. The waitress came over with my usual. After watching

Erica dance to a couple more songs and vaguely listening to Tre and Bran argue about some sports shit, I excused myself to the bathroom. Maintaining eye contact with Erica the whole time. Once inside the bathroom, I waited inside by the door. She came in about 30 seconds later.

"Heeeey Jo. I didn't know you were in here." she pretended.

"Really?" I asked while backing her up to the door, reaching around her and locking it. With her back pressed up against the door, she had nowhere to go. "You didn't see me? Because I definitely saw you." I whispered against her neck while placing small kisses on her collarbone.

"Damn you smell good."

"You told me that already," I said before kissing her lips softly, asking for permission to really kiss her. Erica arched her back, opened her mouth and pulled my head in closer to deepen the

Coming up for breath a few minutes later she

moaned my name. "It's a little early to be calling my name but...." I smiled, dipping down for another kiss.

"Wait...Sam."

"You mean Jo."

"No, I mean what about Sam, Jo?" She said slightly pushing me back. The little bit of distance was what I needed to think clearly.

"Shit." I backed up and leaned on the sink, running my hands through my short curls.

"Jo, I want you. I've wanted you for a while now but we can't do this without Samantha's approval first. She's my best friend and I don't want to hurt her." Erica was still resting on the door and breathing heavily.

"You're right. I would never want to hurt Sam or jeopardize your friendship. I think I should talk to her first. You okay with that?' I asked looking over at Erica and instantly was turned on even more.

"Yeah....I'm okay with that. Jo? Can you do me a favor?"

"Anything."

"Kiss me like that again." Before I could respond she was standing between my legs with her full chest pushed up against mine. I obliged.

I woke up the next morning on the pullout couch in Sam's home office. I rolled over frustrated that I wasn't waking up next to Erica in the guest bedroom. I had to talk to Samantha ASAP. I smelled coffee and heard music playing in the living room and knew my twin was up. Walking out of her office I found her exactly where I knew she would be, sitting on her patio, sipping coffee from her favorite mug. I poured myself a cup and went out to join her.

"Good morning sis," I greeted as I sat down across from her.

"Good morning sissy. How'd you sleep? Sorry I didn't know you were staying over or I would have had Erica sleep with me."

I would rather she sleep with me, I thought to myself.

"I slept okay. You? Is Erica still asleep?"

"Yeah, she's probably hungover."

"Aww damn. I hope it's not too bad. Did you have fun last night?"

"I had a great time. I kicked it with the bouncer for a little while when Erica disappeared. We actually have a little lunch thingy today." Sam slipped in nonchalantly and hid her face in her coffee mug.

"A what? With the bouncer?"

"Jo please let me do this without a big fuss."

"Samantha."

"Come on Jo don't freak out, it's not like that. We're just grabbing a bite to eat, nothing major."

"Who's grabbing a bite to eat?" Erica interrupted as she stepped onto the patio in the smallest pair of boyshorts known to man.

"Me and Rose, the bouncer from the club."

"Hey! I thought we had plans today?" Erica crossed her arms across her chest.

"Shit. Sorry, Erica, it slipped my mind. I'll text her and cancel." Sam reached for her cell phone. I realized this would give me and Erica a chance to spend some time alone together. After that kiss last night we needed to figure out some things. I stopped her before she could finish the text.

"Wait. You don't have to cancel. Me and Erica can hang out while you go on your date."

"It's not a date but really? Why the sudden change of heart?" Sam asked suspiciously.

"I need a favor from you too." I said smiling.

"What kind of favor?"

"I need you to give me and Erica your blessing to date." I thought Erica was going to faint.

"Sam if you aren't okay with this then we will respect that. I don't want to do anything to ruin our friendship or our work relationship. You are too important to me."

Samantha sat quietly for a few minutes while Erica and I looked at each other thinking for sure this was the end of us before there was an us.

"I'll give my blessing on the condition that no matter what happens between you two that you keep me out of it. You are two of the most important people in the world to me and I will not pick sides or lose either one of you. If this doesn't work out then you guys will have to still be amicable to each other. Deal?" Sam looked over at me first and then up at Erica who was still standing by the door.

Erica answered first, "Deal."

"Deal. Thanks, sis."

Sam nodded and got up from the table with her empty coffee cup. "Good! I'm going to get dressed for my....thing."

We both let out a sigh of relief as soon as the door closed. Erica smiled at me suggestively and I shook my head no.

"I meant what I said to Sam. I want to date you, Erica, not just sleep with you. I want to see if there's more than just sexual tension between us. So get dressed. We're going on a date thing too," I got up from the table and kissed a shocked Erica on the forehead before going into the house.

ERICA

---◁♦▷---

Am I really going on a date with Jo? What the hell am I getting myself into? I'm not gay…..well I don't know what I am. Especially after that damn kiss last night. I think I'm still wet. It's not like I've had any male prospects lately. She is so damn sexy and she is sweet. I was expecting her to jump in my pants after Samantha gave her blessing but for Jo to say she actually wants to date and take it slow makes me think. Maybe I should give this a serious chance. If she's willing to then why not? Right?

All these thoughts and more ran through my mind as I showered and got dressed to go hang out with Jo. She left right after our encounter on the patio and promised to be back in an hour. I wanted to look cute but not like I was trying too hard. I was glad I had packed two outfits, I put on some dark ripped jeans with a green crop top and tan sandals. I put my blonde braids in a ponytail, a touch of mascara, lipstick and gold hoops. I smiled at my reflection in the full-length mirror in Samantha's guest room. I walked into the hallway and ran into Samantha coming out of her room wearing a cute pink and white halter sundress.

"Ooh you look cute for your non-date," I said smiling and putting my hands on my hips.

Samantha laughed, "are you going to give me a hard time about this too? Do I look overdressed?"

"How can I give you a hard time about something you didn't even tell me about?" I said making a face and rolling my eyes.

"I'm sorry boo. We were all a little tipsy last night and I planned on talking to you this morning but then I got hit with an unexpected question."

"Oh yeah…..about that. You know I didn't plan for this to happen. Not that anything has happened. I guess you could say it was more than just a crush there. Or that's what we want to see. I'm honestly a little shocked myself. I wasn't expecting…."

"Erica, it's okay," Samantha cut me off before I could really get to rambling, "I'm not mad. I knew you both were crushing on each other. It was only a matter of time before you two stopped avoiding the inevitable and see where this could lead. I'm actually excited. If this works out, then we'll really be sisters!"

"Whoa too fast!" I said, taking a step back and giggling. "Wait, did you say BOTH crushing? You mean Jo had a crush on me and you knew and didn't say anything?! Samantha!"

Samantha took off down the stairs, laughing and yelled back up at me, "I think I heard the door."

"You did not hear the door. I want an answer!" I chased her into the kitchen.

"Erica I can explain," Samantha put her hands up to surrender.

"What are we explaining?" Jo entered the kitchen looking sexy as hell with a pair of dark sunglasses on.

I licked my lips which caused her to smile and peek over her sunglasses, looking me up and down. She moved towards me, I assumed to give me a kiss.

"Not so fast. How long have you had a crush on me?" I asked and backed up just out of arm's reach.

Jo looked at Samantha and she ducked out of the kitchen yelling "I'm going to be late! Talk to you guys later!" I heard her keys jingling and then the front door closing.

I stood there waiting for Jo to answer my question. "Well?" I added impatiently.

"Well...remember when you colored your hair to this honey-blonde color?"

"What? Jo, my hair has been this color since you met me how many years ago?" I put my hands on my hips.

"Exactly."

With that one word I kissed her the way she kissed me last night. She picked me up and put me on the counter so effortlessly I forgot she was a damn female. I ran my fingers through her curls while she gripped my ass. "I want you so bad," I said against her lips when we came up for air.

"I want you too" she replied kissing my neck "but not yet. I want to do this right."

"Then why are you playing with my emotions and my ear right now."

"You're right. I'm sorry." Jo tried to back away but I wrapped my legs around her waist and held her in place. I draped my arms across her shoulders and stared into her eyes.

"What are we doing Jo?"

"Erica...you've known me for a while now. I've been crushing on you since damn near the first day we met but you were off-limits for obvious reasons. Then the timing was never right. You was dating ol' boy then I was in a relationship with Monica. Plus you were straight....even though I'm sure I could have turned you years ago," she paused and leaned in to lick my neck causing me to shudder and prove her point, "honestly, other than our harmless flirting I didn't think you were interested. My sisters' friends have always liked me. Last night though....last night I realized maybe I should make a move. I figured if you shot me down I'd pretend to be drunk and we could laugh about it later. But I told myself if you were serious then I wanted to actually date you and get to know you better not just get between your legs...."

"Yet here you are between my legs." I stopped her and reached in for a kiss. This kiss was different from the others. Not as deep and sensual yet just as passionate. When we broke free I decided it was my turn to talk. "I realized I had a little more than a crush on you about a year ago after you and Monica broke up. I saw a different side of you while you were going through that and I remember thinking how stupid she was for hurting you and that I would have appreciated and loved you the way she should have. I know you're a little nervous because I've never really been with a woman but I promise to keep it a hundred with you at all times. I'm not entertaining anyone else and I really want to see where this takes us. But if you're saying no sex then you're going to have to stop looking and smelling so damn good in my presence. Maybe stop showering or something." I laughed and uncrossed my legs from behind her allowing her to move.

Jo tilted her head to the side with a confused look on her face. "Who said anything about no sex?" She sucked lightly on my bottom lip before stepping back and winking. She was out of the kitchen before I could catch my breath. "Let's go, woman, we're already behind schedule!" I hopped off the counter and took a deep breath before heading to the front door where she was waiting, smiling. I rolled my eyes at her, attempting to seem aggravated as I walked by, she tapped me on the butt, "did I tell you that you look sexy today?" I smiled to myself, walking to the elevator while she locked up Samantha's apartment.

"Where are you taking me?" I asked as we exited the elevator and walked towards her truck.

"It's a surprise." She opened the door for me and walked around to the driver's side.

"Okay." I reached over to turn the radio on and realized she was staring at me. "What?"

"You're not going to ask any other questions? Just 'okay'?"

"You said it was a surprise. Do you want me to ask questions?" I was a little confused.

"No not at all. I'm just kind of surprised but okay." Jo responded and backed out of her parking spot.

"You'll learn real quick Josephine that I'm not like any other woman you've ever dated." She cut her eyes at me for calling me by her full name but didn't say anything. As she jumped on the highway her right hand slid over and rested on my thigh. I smiled while asking myself for the umpteenth time in less than 24 hours What am I getting myself into? Oh well, fuck it. With that last thought, I entwined my fingers with hers and got comfortable in my seat. I might as well enjoy the ride.

I must have dozed off during the ride because when I woke up the truck was parked and Jo was gone. It looked like we were at a park somewhere. I got out and looked around trying to figure out where the hell my date was. At that moment she appeared from over a hill. She smiled as she approached me. She must have seen my face because she immediately put her hands on my arms once she reached me and said, "relax I was only gone for five minutes. You were sleeping so peacefully that I didn't want to wake you right away so I went to get set up first." She pecked me on the lips a couple of times until I finally caved.

"Okay, okay but someone could have kidnapped me," I said, only half-joking with my bottom lip poked out.

"Not on my watch. They would have to go through me first." She kissed me again, this time a little more than a peck and I fully relaxed. "Are you ready for our date?" She asked while studying my face to make sure I was really okay.

"Yes, I'm ready." I smiled and returned a quick kiss to prove it. She hit a button on her key fob that turned the truck off and then locked the doors. We walked hand in hand over the hill she had just come from a few minutes ago. When we reached the top I could see a picnic laid out in the shade of a tree. There was a blanket spread out on the ground along with a couple of pillows and another blanket, a picnic basket, and two wine glasses.

"This is really cute Jo!" I gushed as we got closer. Once seated, she opened the basket and pulled out some of my favorite foods. My favorite wine was first, grapes and strawberries, merlot cheese and crackers, turtle cheesecake and a bouquet of Stargazer lilies.

"Jo….I don't know what to say to all of this. How did you know about these things?"

"What do you mean, how did I know?" She was filling the wine glasses and looked over at me clearly confused. She handed me a glass and put the bottle down. "Seriously Erica? I've known you for six years now. I think I know you a little bit. Whenever Samantha has an event or a girl's night you bring a bottle of this wine and the merlot cheese even though you prefer sweet wine you like the contrast of the flavors. You always order the cheesecake. Sam even gets it for you as a peace offering when she's being too bossy."

"And the flowers?" I asked my voice barely above a whisper. I was beyond amazed at how much she had paid attention to me over the years.

"Those? I cheated and asked Sam." She laughed at herself.

"Wow Jo. No one has ever done anything like this for me before. I'm really touched. Thank you."

"You my dear have clearly been dating the wrong people because this is just the beginning." She leaned over with a strawberry in hand. Once I bit into it she followed up with a kiss making it even sweeter.

We drank, talked, ate and laughed until it started getting dark. We packed the empty containers back into the picnic basket and folded the blankets. Walking back to the truck I thought about how perfect the afternoon had been. Jo opened the passenger door for me and put the items in the trunk before getting in on the driver's side.

"Dare I ask what you have planned next?" I asked as she started the engine.

"Will you stay the night with me?" She asked looking into my soul. I nodded and leaned over to kiss her.

The drive to Jo's place was quiet but not in an awkward way. I made sure to text Samantha to let her know I wasn't coming back to her place so she wouldn't wait up. I asked if she wanted to have breakfast in the morning so we could swap date stories. She responded with a thumbs up and a kissy face. I hoped her date was going as well as mine. When I looked up we had arrived at Jo's condo, she opened my door as usual and escorted me to the front door. Once inside she asked if I wanted something to drink. I told her a glass of wine would be nice.

I called out to Jo in the kitchen, "do you mind if I take a quick shower? I smell like outside."

"Of course not. Use my bathroom, there are towels in the closet and t-shirts in…" she stopped mid-sentence when she got to the kitchen doorway. I was standing there wearing nothing but my matching bra and panties. "Damn…Erica…I" she stumbled over her words.

"Jo, I know what you said about dating and getting to know each other and I can appreciate that but as you said earlier, we've known each other for six years now. So while we see where this takes us I want to fully enjoy the ride. Okay?" She nodded, unable to take her eyes off me and for once not able to speak.

"Good. I'm going to shower and depending on where you want it, I'll either meet you in the bedroom or back down here in 15 minutes." I walked away slowly and super happy with the fact I decided to put on a thong today. I didn't have to turn around to know that Jo was staring at my ass and probably drooling. Once in Jo's bathroom, I closed the door and leaned up against it trying to catch my breath. I looked at myself in the mirror over the sink. Am I really about to do this? I damn sure am, I whispered under my breath.

When I got out of the shower, I wrapped a towel around me and opened the door, entering Jo's bedroom. There was soft music playing and candles lit but no Jo. I sat down on the edge of the bed and started lotioning my legs with a bottle on her nightstand.

"Why don't you let me do that?" I looked up and she was in the doorway. She had changed into a pair of black basketball shorts with a white tank top and her hair was wet, I assumed from showering. I couldn't help but wish she had joined me in the shower. She walked over to me, took the lotion from me and as if she had read my mind she said, "next time we can conserve water and shower together." She sat on the king-sized bed next to me, put my feet in her lap and began lotioning and massaging my feet. She inched up my calves and thighs, lotioning and massaging the whole way. As she got higher and higher, I closed my eyes and leaned my head back. When she reached the bottom of my towel, she stopped. I opened my eyes and she was staring at me.

"God, you're beautiful." She said, causing me to blush and smile. She eased me back on the bed, pulling my towel open at the same time. With my body fully exposed, she hovered over me, I closed my eyes, preparing for a kiss, instead, Jo sucked my right nipple into her mouth slowly. I arched my back and moaned out loud. It felt like her mouth and hands were all over my body at the same time. She licked and sucked my breasts until I came...hard. The room was spinning and I tried to catch my breath but then I felt her kissing her way down my stomach. Before I could begin to protest, Jo was licking my clit like a cat drinking milk. My body was tingling everywhere and then I passed out. No, not really but it damn sure felt like an outer body experience. The next thing I remember was her pulling the covers over us both as she spooned behind me and kissed my neck, "goodnight my luv." She whispered as I drifted off to sleep. My last thought was - I will be getting her back for this in the morning. As soon as I can feel my legs again.

SAMANTHA

I sat in the parking lot of the restaurant trying to get up the nerve to go inside. I saw Rose when she pulled up and walked to the front. She checked her watch and phone, I assumed to see if I had texted her. I studied her from a distance and realized she was even cuter than I could tell last night. She was taller than me, maybe 5'11, a muscular build, dark-skinned, long straight hair that she wore in a ponytail. She was wearing jeans, gray Adidas and a matching Adidas t-shirt. I contemplated just leaving and texting her that I was sick or that something came up but then my phone dinged with a text.

```
Erica: Have fun on your non-date
boo! Can't wait to swap stories
tonight. Thanks again for being
okay with me and Jo. She really is
something.
```

That gave me the courage I needed. I turned off my engine and opened the door before I could change my mind. Rose looked up as I got closer and smiled, showing her dimples and perfect white teeth. She looked genuinely happy to see me, I smiled back. When I reached her, she embraced me and said, "Hey baby girl. I thought you stood me up."

"Hey, I'm barely five minutes late," my hand rested on her upper arm after we broke away, "sorry I…"

"No need to explain. You're here now and that's all that matters." She smiled and opened the door for me. I smiled back and walked inside of the restaurant she chose for lunch.

"You look really pretty." She said after we were seated.

"Thank you." I blushed a little.

"Did you sleep okay? I hope I didn't keep you on the phone too late."

"I did and I enjoyed talking to you. It's been forever since I fell asleep on the phone." I laughed.

"Yeah, me too."

"Samantha? Hey stranger!" I recognized the voice before I saw her, Darrin's best friend's fiancé Kelly. She was coming towards the table with her sister Bianca, so I got up and plastered a fake smile on my face. Kelly gave me a big hug and started chatting away about her and Robert's destination wedding plans. She was so busy talking that she hadn't noticed Rose. I saw "the look" on her face for a quick second when she did see her. She recovered quickly but I definitely saw it.

"Kelly, Bianca, let me introduce you to my really good friend Rose. Rose, this is Kelly and her sister Bianca. Kelly's fiancé and Darrin are best friends." I purposely dropped Darrin's name so they wouldn't get too suspicious, besides Rose knew all about Darrin. We were on the phone for hours last night talking and I was completely honest with her about him and everything.

"Nice to meet you, ladies." Rose said as she stood up to shake their hands.

"You too. Samantha, are you guys coming to dinner tomorrow? We can catch up on everything." Kelly barely acknowledged Rose before turning her attention right back to me which kind of pissed me off. Bianca at least smiled at Rose, or was that a smirk?

"I don't know. I'll have Darrin call Robert if we are coming." I responded icily.

"Oh….okay. Well, enjoy. I'll talk to you later." She smiled slightly, waved at Rose and walked away.

"Nice meeting you Rose. See you around, Samantha." Bianca followed her sister.

I waited until they were completely gone before sitting back down. When I looked at Rose, she had the biggest grin on her face.

"What's that smile all about?" I asked puzzled.

"Nothing at all baby girl. Shall we continue our date."

"Sure…...and it's…."

"Not a date. I know. We're just really good friends." She was still smiling at me with those dimples.

"Are you mocking me?" I asked only half-serious.

"Absolutely not. I wouldn't dare do such a thing." Rose stopped smiling but you could still hear the laughter in her voice.

"Anyway, I feel like we talked about me all last night so I want to talk about you."

"Okay. What do you want to know?"

"Everything? What was your childhood like? Are your parents still together? How long have you been a detective? What's your sign? Favorite color?"

"Okay, okay. Someone's had too much caffeine this morning." Rose laughed and put her hand over mine on the table to stop my twenty questions. Something about that touch sent a shiver up my back and I looked at her hand on mine. She pulled back apologizing.

"No that's okay. Listen can we get out of here?"

"Is everything okay? We haven't even ordered yet." Rose looked confused and concerned.

I flashed her a smile, "Yeah, I'm good. I was just thinking we can go somewhere a little less formal. I mean if that's okay with you?"

"Whatever you want to do. I don't care where we go as long as we're together," she got up from the table and pulled my chair back.

"Laying it on kind of thick, huh?" I joked as I stood up.

She smiled, bent down and whispered in my ear, "you ain't seen nothing yet." I blushed and shivered again when I felt her breath on my ear.

We dropped my car off at Rose's house since she lived closer to the restaurant. I hopped in the front seat of her Audi. We decided to go to the mall and walk around. I was craving a Cinnabon and I needed a new book to read. I was completely caught by surprise to find out we read a lot of the same books. We debated the whole way there about if the Crossfire series was better than 50 Shades. I felt so completely at ease with her. I found myself touching her arm a lot when talking. Finally, she grabbed my hand and held it on her lap, "if you keep touching me like that I'm going to kiss you and I promised myself I wasn't going to do that."

"Oh...sorry. I didn't mean to...." I responded quietly.

"It's okay. Just me being honest." She looked at me for a quick second.

"What if I asked you to?"

"To kiss you? I don't know Samantha. I like you and I'm cool with us being friends while you figure stuff out but I'm not trying to get hurt in the process. I hope you understand."

"Of course I understand. Forget I said anything. I'm sorry." I mumbled feeling bad for even being here with her and not knowing what I wanted.

"Stop apologizing." She pulled into a parking spot and turned to face me. She gently grabbed my face and turned it towards her. She leaned over and kissed me, softly all while holding my face.

"You ready to get that Cinnabon?" She asked after pulling away, searching my face to see if she made a mistake. I smiled and nodded since I felt like I couldn't speak. I felt that kiss all the way in my toes. Oh...Jesus if that was just a kiss…..

On the way back to Rose's house to get my car, Erica texted to say that she was going to stay the night with Jo and asked if we could grab breakfast in the morning. I texted back a thumbs up and a kissy face but I was a little sad that I was going home alone. I wanted to hear about their date and tell her about our afternoon at the mall. Rose opened the passenger door to let me out of her car. She held my hand as she walked me to mine.

"What you and Erica got planned for the rest of the evening?" she asked standing way too close to me as I leaned back against the car door and looked up at her.

"She's staying the night at my sister's," I responded as nonchalantly as I could muster.

"Oh...you want to hang out here for a little while? I promise to behave." she wiggled her eyebrows up and down sillily.

I giggled at her and playfully pushed her back, "where's the fun in that?"

She grabbed my hand and walked backwards up the driveway towards the house, still wiggling her eyebrows and smiling mischievously.

After giving me a tour of her 2 story 4 bedroom home, she asked if I wanted some clothes to change into. I nodded and she went into her closet. She emerged a couple of minutes later with a pair of sweatpants and a t-shirt. She left me in the bedroom to change and went downstairs to mix us some drinks. I smiled into her shirt as I inhaled the scent that was her. I pulled it over my head onto my skin and imagined it was her touching me. I folded my dress and laid it on the bench at the foot of the bed. As I walked into the living room, Rose was coming out of the kitchen with 2 drinks on a tray with a bowl of popcorn.

"I thought I was going to have to come find you. You look even cuter than you did earlier," she looked me up and down and I felt like I didn't have any clothes on at all.

"Ummm so what are we watching? I sat on the couch and pulled a blanket off the back to cover my lap. Rose sat the tray on the ottoman in front of us, handed me the remote and sat next to me.

"Whatever you want. I'm not picky." She handed me my drink and pulled the blanket on her lap with the bowl of popcorn. I flipped the channels and decided on the old show Friends. I glanced at her to gauge her reaction.

"I love this show. Which character are you?"

She continued to surprise me, "I'm Rachel. You?"

"Joey."

"Oh really? So you're a ladies man? Well, not man but….you know what I mean." I laughed at myself.

"Joey wasn't always a ladies man. He also fell for a girl he couldn't have and went through the pain of just being friends while she was with someone else."

"Oh...yeah."

Rose chuckled, "Relax. I wasn't talking about you."

"Oh good!" I laughed nervously.

We watched a couple of episodes, chatting in between commercials. She told me about her 1st love, which was her best friend and roommate in college. She was straight and did not have the same feelings for Rose but she used her for whatever she needed including sex.

"So you make it a habit of saving us confused girls, huh?" I tried to lighten the mood.

"Kind of…." Rose got up and went to refill her cup.

I put my head in my hand and mumbled 'shit' under my breath. She was such a sweetheart. The last thing I wanted to do was lead her on and hurt her the way Gloria did. I got off the couch and went into the kitchen.

"Rose, maybe I should go…."

She turned around and she seemed angry.

"I don't want to hurt you. I shouldn't be here. I don't want to get you mixed up in my drama and confusion. I'm sorry." It was all I could do not to cry.

"No, it's not you, it's just that I've never told anyone about Gloria. I always blamed myself and thought I wasn't good enough for her."

"Fuck her. You were too good for her and it's her loss, not yours." I moved closer to her.

"Am I too good for you too?" She whispered.

"Probably," I whispered back, stood on my tippy toes and kissed her. It started sweet and almost innocent but quickly deepened into more. She pulled me into her body and wrapped her arms around my waist.

"Sorry," I whispered after the kiss ended.

"Stop apologizing." She smiled and caressed my cheek. "Look, Samantha, I'm a big girl. Not the same kid that fell for Gloria. I am walking into this….friendship with my eyes wide open. I don't want you to do anything that you'll regret. I'm here for you in whatever capacity you need me to be. So no more apologies. Okay?"

"Okay….I just…"

Rose kissed me and stopped whatever I was going to say. "Why don't we go back to Friends?"

"We are friends…"

"The show woman ." Rose laughed at me, grabbed my hand and her drink as we walked back to the couch. We stayed up for hours watching Friends, talking about life, a couple more stolen kisses later and I was asleep in her arms on the couch.

JOSEPHINE

---◁◆▷---

I rolled over just as the sun was coming up and snuggled closer to Erica, still in disbelief that she was in my bed. I'm glad I finally made a move but damn how much time did I waste? I want to take it slow but at the same time, I don't want to waste one more second. I've had feelings for her for quite some time now but never in a million years did I think she might feel the same way. I had my days when it was "fun" messing with straight or curious girls. It was a challenge but after a while, that shit got tiresome and lonely. Eventually, after their curiosity was satisfied, they were right back playing for their home team. That's what had kept me from Erica for so long but damn I hope she's different. Laying with my arms wrapped around her waist, her scent still on my lips felt like heaven. Just then she stirred and rolled over to face me.

"Good morning beautiful," I caressed her face.

"Good morning," she smiled shyly.

"You feel okay?"

"I don't know. I think I'm still having an outer body experience. Whatever you did to me was totally unfair. We're not on an equal playing field." she attempted to scowl at me.

"Why aren't we?" I laughed.

"Don't laugh. I'm serious. Because I'm a little inexperienced in this area."

"You're inexperienced in the bedroom?"

"Well….no…but….I've never had sex with a woman before. It's different."

"How so? Because if you prefer a penis, I can go get one out of the closet." I said completely straight-faced as I moved to get out of bed.

"Jo!" She pulled me back. "No, I don't want a penis, but I want to be able to pleasure you the way you pleased me last night." I could tell she was serious.

"One step at a time baby. Come here." I lay on my back and motioned for Erica to straddle me. Once on top, I could tell she was wet and I closed my eyes. "Damn girl," I half-whispered, half moaned.

"You can feel that?"

She started rocking her hips back and forth, slowly at first and then picking up the pace a little. I gripped her hips tight in response. She leaned forward, placing her hands on the pillow on either side of my head and bent down to kiss me. Our breathing sped up as we were both chasing a high, she rode me like her life depended on it and I held on like my life did too. I could sense she was close and I was only waiting on her so I slapped her hard on the ass, sending her over the edge, dragging me with her. Several minutes later after I caught my breath,

"I'm cooking breakfast. What you want?"

She started laughing, "oh I put it down to the point that you going to cook me breakfast?"

"Actually, it's a tie so we need some energy before we have a tie-breaker." I laughed back while slowly stroking her back.

"Uhh uhh!" She yelled and rolled off me and the bed, landing on her feet on the floor. "You're not going to turn me into a Jo addict. Besides I promised Sam we could have breakfast. I feel bad for leaving her last night."

"But it's still early," I whined and reached for her as she skirted out of my reach and ran in the bathroom giggling. I laid back down and sighed.

"Hey Jo! Remember what you said about water conservation?" Erica called from the shower. I jumped up and ran in the bathroom.

A couple hours later we pulled into Samantha's parking deck and I noticed her car wasn't there. "Have you talked to Sam today? Where she at so early?" I asked Erica.

"Last I heard from her was last night when I told her I was staying with you."

"Did she say where she was?"

"No, I didn't ask. I'll text her."

"That's ok I'll call her." I hit a couple of buttons on the dash of my truck and then you could hear the phone ringing. After a couple rings, an unfamiliar, groggy female voice answered.

"Hello?"

"Where's my sister?" I said through clenched teeth.

"Samantha, Jo's on the phone," I heard Sam mutter 'shit' under her breath before getting on the phone.

"Hey Jo."

"Don't 'hey Jo' me. What the hell Samantha?! You don't even know this chick and you already laid up at her house and…."

"I'm not in the mood for a lecture right now. I'll be home soon…"

"Oh but you gonna get a damn lecture. Just cause she a female don't mean shit. You can still be a ho…." I heard Erica gasp and I knew I had gone too far. "Sam I d…"

"How about you not be at my house when I get there Josephine?" I could hear the emotion in her voice before she hung up.

"Shit!"

"If she's acting like a ho then what does that make me?" Erica demanded reaching for the door handle.

"Erica wait! I didn't mean that besides it's not the same, we know each other. Sam just met her two days ago and she already…."

"Already what? Jo you and I both know Samantha didn't sleep with Rose. She's not even like that."

"Yeah, I know Sam's not like that but I also know cats like Rose. They prey on confused, curious girls like Sam, sleep with them and kick them to the curb. I just don't want to see my sister get hurt."

"   Confused, curious girls like me?"

"Come on Erica stop trying to twist my words. We're not them!"

"You're right, we're not them but me and Samantha are both grown-ass women. Whatever we decide to do with our body is our choice, not yours, Rose's or anyone else. Okay?"

"Okay, I'm sorry. I didn't mean it like that. You still gonna let me touch your body with my body?" I asked, hoping to lighten the mood a little.

"Don't try to get cute Jo."

"But I'm already cute. For real babe, I'm sorry. I didn't mean to upset you or Samantha. I promise I'll make it right when she gets here."

"Ummm did you not hear her say don't be here? She was serious and I'd hate for her to kill you so soon after we just started dating. Besides, we might have to jump you cause you all Army strong and shit."

"Air Force…."

"I know what damn branch you in but they don't have a slogan. Jo if you correct me…"

I closed my mouth and kept my smart comment to myself. "Okay I'll leave. The last thing I want is to have you both upset with me. Will you apologize to her for me?" I grabbed her hand and brought it to my lips.

"Who said I was on your side?" She narrowed her eyes and tried to pull her hand back.

"Oooh girl you sexy when you get mad. Let's fight so we can make up later," I teased, kissing her hand and massaging her thigh at the same time.

"Bye Jo," she pulled her hand away and opened the door. Before she got out she leaned over and kissed me, "I'll call you later. If you're good, then I'll take you to dinner."

"Well you already know I'm good so what time should I be ready?" I teased.

Erica rolled her eyes, "bye Jo."

I watched her walk into the building before pulling out my phone and sending a text to Tre and Bran -

```
Jo: Who hired the new bouncer at the
club? What do we know about her? Meet
me at my crib in 30.
```

I turned my music up and sped out of the garage. I did not want to run into Sam until I knew more about Rose.

SAMANTHA

I can't believe Jo just called me a ho. As if I didn't already feel some type of way about staying the night at Rose's house. Even though we slept on the couch and didn't do anything…..well we kissed….a lot. I touched my lips and smiled in the mirror over the sink. A knock on the bathroom door jolted me out of my inappropriate thoughts.

"Samantha? You ok in there?" Rose asked from the other side of the door. I checked my face to make sure it didn't look like I had been crying before opening the door.

"I'm fine! I think I'm gonna head out though," I smiled at her, hoping she didn't pry too much.

"You don't have to front with me. I heard what Jo said to you. You want to talk about it."

No such luck.

"It's no big deal. She's always been overprotective. She takes those 4 minutes real serious." I laughed, she didn't.

"Listen I don't want to get involved in family issues because it's not my place but I don't like to see you upset." She moved closer to me and brushed my hair behind my ear. "I get being overprotective and I don't blame her. You're gorgeous and it's a lot of crazy people out here. But still…."

"Don't worry about it. I'll curse her out, she'll apologize and we'll be good in a couple days."

"That doesn't make it right or healthy Samantha…."

"Rose, please drop it. I don't want to fight with you too."

"Okay. I'm sorry. I don't want to fight with you either." She pulled me to her, kissed me softly before wrapping her arms around me. I hugged her back, exhaling deep, letting the tension melt away. We stood like that for a couple of minutes in complete silence.

"Thank you," I mumbled into her shirt.

"For what?"

"For not pressuring me into anything last night. For knowing that I'm a complete mess yet still holding me like I am the only girl in the world."

"Samantha, you are not a complete mess. I meant what I said about being here in whatever capacity you need me to be. I'm okay with being your friend while you figure things out. And I promise if that changes, I'll let you know as long as you do the same. Deal?" She leaned away from me so she could see my face.

"Deal." I didn't even know what I was agreeing to but I knew I liked the way I felt with her. I haven't felt the way I felt in the last 24 hours in almost a year. I needed to explore this feeling more.

And we did for the next several months. We fell asleep on the phone together almost every night. I stayed at her house maybe once a week and we went out every weekend. It was hard balancing time with her and time with Darrin but so far it was working.

When we finally landed the Harris account at work, Rose was the 1st person I called. Erica wanted to go out to celebrate but of course Jo was coming and I still wasn't really speaking to her. She'd apologized profusely, Erica begged me to forgive her, even Rose tried to speak on her behalf after they had some type of "stud to stud" talk but I wasn't ready yet. She really hurt my feelings and I needed her to feel it. So, I turned Erica down and decided to let Rose take me out instead. I called Darrin and told him I was going out to celebrate with Erica and our team from the office. He was happy for us and agreed that we could go out for breakfast the next day.

Just as I finished my makeup, the doorbell rang. Rose was always right on time. I opened the door to a bouquet of Calla Lilies and those dimples. "You look amazing!" Rose said as she kissed me and handed me the flowers. I was wearing a backless red dress with a pair of silver strappy sandals.

"These flowers are amazing! Thank you!" I exclaimed.

"You ready to hit the town?"

"Yeah let me put these in water and grab my bag. Come in." I held the door open for her and walked to the kitchen. "Where are you taking me?" I yelled.

"I got a section at this new lounge downtown. Is that ok?"

"Of course that's okay as long as it isn't one of my sister's clubs."

"When are you going to forgive her?"

I rounded the corner with my purse, "what happened to not being healthy and normal?" I put my hands on my hips.

Rose sighed before answering, " I know what I said but the last thing I wanted was for you to cut her out of your life Samantha. I know you miss her."

"I do miss her and I haven't cut her out. I just needed some time. I'll reach out....soon."

"Okay, whatever you say babe." Rose shrugged her shoulders.

"I say let's go celebrate." I walked towards the front door.

"As you wish." Rose bowed at the waist and held the door open for me, causing me to giggle.

When we arrived at the club, Rose gave a name to the bouncer who let us right in. Once inside we were escorted to our section which was upstairs overlooking the dance floor. It was decorated with 'Congratulations" balloons and there was already a bottle of champagne and champagne flutes on the table.

"Oooh baby thank you!" I gave her a kiss on the cheek as she poured my glass.

"I want to toast to the smartest, sexiest, most beautiful woman here. I'm proud of you and I know there will be many more moments for us to celebrate in the future." I knew there was more to the last line in Rose's toast and I hoped she was right.

"Here's to great friends and…."

"Family" A familiar voice said behind me. I turned to see my big sister Charlotte holding a champagne flute.

"Charlie!! AAAAH!! Oh my God, what are you doing here?!" I jumped up and down as she walked from around the back of the couch. She put her glass on the table before hugging me, otherwise I would have knocked it out of her hand. I was so happy to see her. It had been a little more than six months since her, her husband and my niece moved to be closer to his new job. Even though they were only a couple of hours away, life makes it seem further when you get busy.

"What do you mean, what am I doing here? A little birdie with cute dimples told me there was a reason to celebrate so where else would I be besides with my baby sister?"

"Rose? You did this? For me? How did you….." I looked at her in complete wonder before giving her a big hug and kiss.

"Ahem. Do you guys want to be alone?" Charlie asked only half-joking. It suddenly dawned on me that Charlie didn't know about my 'curiosity' or the fact that Rose was a little more than a friend.

"Sorry, I got a little carried away." I wiped my lips as I let Rose loose and picked up my champagne glass.

"I see. Rose it's great to finally meet you in person." Charlie embraced Rose.

"Likewise," Rose replied with a smile.

"Where's Jo?" Charlie asked as she picked up her glass and sat down.

I cut my eyes over at Rose. If Charlie found out we weren't speaking, she would have both of our asses. Rose answered before I could make up something.

"She should be here momentarily. She was valeting her car a minute ago."

"Oh okay. I was about to say it's not like her to miss such a big moment for Sam."

"What am I missing besides my beautiful big sister?" Jo appeared at the right moment, as always.

"Hey, my Jo-Jo!" Charlie exclaimed, jumping up to hug Jo. Erica slid around them and hugged me, she whispered in my ear, "I promise I had no idea we were meeting up with you guys. Don't be mad at me."

"I'm not mad. Besides I know this was all the work of my 'Knight in Shining Armor' over there." I gestured towards Rose who was grinning from ear to ear. Erica smiled at Rose and headed over to hug Charlie while Jo went around to dap and hug Rose. Suddenly we were facing each other.

"Hey, Sam." She said, looking a little nervous.

"Hey, Jo." I broke out in a smile, genuinely happy to see my twin. She returned the smile and opened her arms as if she was asking for a hug. I hugged her tightly realizing just how much I had missed her.

"Since we are all here together. I have an announcement to make. Thank you guys for coming out to celebrate tonight. The account we just acquired is going to make my firm a lot of money but we couldn't have done it without my right hand. Erica you are the main reason this even happened. So, I think it's only right that you be the one to handle the account as the associate in charge and not as my assistant. You are being promoted."

"What?! Oh my...thank you Samantha! This means so much to me. I promise I won't let you down!"

"Congratulations Erica!" Everyone cheered and held up their glass.

"Congratulation's baby!" Jo swung Erica around and planted a big kiss on her.

The waitress came over asking if we wanted another bottle of champagne. Rose, Jo, and Charlie all answered 'yes' at the same time. This was going to be a great night. Somewhere in between bottles, Charlie announced to Erica and Rose that they were going home alone because we were having a sister's sleepover. Normally I would have been a little disappointed but I was so excited to have both of my sisters in my presence it didn't even bother me. Besides, we had so much catching up to do that we would need more than just a one-night sleepover.

CHARLOTTE

We were outside of the lounge waiting for the valet to bring the cars around. The plan was that Erica would drive Jo's truck home so that Jo and Sam could ride with me back to Sam's place. I was actually a little surprised that Jo agreed to that suggestion, considering how much she loved her truck. That either showed some maturity on my little sister's side or how much she cared for and trusted Erica. I was leaning towards the latter.

Jo's truck pulled up first and Erica hopped in the driver's seat. Jo leaned in the window, kissed Erica, told her to be careful and asked her to text when she made it home safe. Erica agreed and yelled one last goodbye to us before she pulled off.

"This is niiiiice," I said in my Tiffany Haddish voice as the valet pulled Rose's cream on cream Audi to the curb.

She laughed and thanked me. She wrapped her arms around Sam's waist and pulled her in for an embrace. Sam gave her a quick kiss on the lips with a promise to call her tomorrow.

It looked like both of my sisters were happy but I definitely had some questions for Sam about Darrin. When Rose called me to tell me about Sam's celebration and to mention that her and Jo weren't talking, she only mentioned that she and Sam were friends. It was clear that there was a little more to that friendship than she let on. Rose shook Jo's hand and gave me a hug before getting in her car and leaving. Finally, the valet pulled up in my red Camry. Jo insisted on driving and we were on our way.

An hour later we were all in our pj's sitting on Sam's couch with wine and snacks. As much as I wanted to jump into what was going on with my life I decided to hear from them first.

"How did you and Erica come about?"

"I don't know. It just kind of happened, I guess. I was feeling her for a while…."

"We know!" Me and Sam cut her off and started giggling.

"What you mean? How did y'all know?" Jo demanded.

"Let's see…. besides your continued flirting…." Samantha started.

"That's normal. I flirt with everybody." Jo said defensively.

"And the way you smiled whenever she came around or I mentioned her name. Oh and let's not forget how you hated the guy she was dating a couple years ago."

"I hated him because he was an asshole and not good enough for her. And I was right."

"You were right but I don't know how much your ex-girlfriend agreed with that opinion considering you used to say it all the time in front of her!" Samantha said as she started laughing again

"I...whatever. I'm going to refill my glass." Jo got up and semi-stomped into the kitchen.

"Just bring the bottle!" I yelled and tried not to snicker.

"Yeah, yeah, yeah". She yelled back.

She came back a few seconds later with two bottles of wine and an opener.

"Can I finish my story now?" She asked as she topped off everyone's glass.

"By all means." I answered around a mouthful of popcorn.

"As I was saying before I was rudely interrupted." Jo looked at Samantha expecting a rebuttal but Sam 'zipped' her lips and didn't say another word. "I had been feeling her for a while but I didn't think it was a good idea. One because of their friendship and two I didn't think she was interested. Then one night we were going out and I sensed a vibe from her that she might be a little curious so I decided to make a move. We asked Samantha for her blessing to see where it could lead and the rest is history."

"Well, considering she had a girlfriend in college, I think it's safe to say she was more than a little curious, although she claims that was just a phase. Plus she's been crushing on you for a little while too." Samantha shrugged her shoulders casually as she made that revelation.

"Wait….what? How come you never told me that before now?!"

"The girlfriend thing was not my business to tell. And you were in a whole relationship with someone else so why would I tell you that Erica had a crush on you? Besides, what difference does it make now? You found your way to each other."

"What you mean what difference does it make?! Things might have been….."

"Okay, hold on!" I could see this was about to turn ugly so I decided to intervene before our sister's night was cut short before it even started. "Jo, I think what Samantha is trying to say is that the timing wasn't right. No one knew how things would turn out between you and Monica." I saw her calm down a little.

"Exactly and I wouldn't insert myself into your life and relationship that way."

I could tell by the way Jo winced a little that Samantha's statement had a double meaning. I decided to let it go for now. It would come out before the night was over.

"You're right. Sometimes I just wish Erica and I had started dating earlier and I hadn't wasted so much time on people who didn't deserve it. I think I want to ask her to be exclusive. I'm not thinking about anyone else and I want to focus on getting to know each other better."

"I think Erica would really like that." Samantha smiled and nodded at Jo.

"On to you little sister. Care to tell me when you and Darrin broke up? And when did you start dating women?" I turned my attention and my body towards Samantha.

"Darrin and I are still together. And Rose and I are just friends." Sam stated matter of factly.

"I'm confused...." I started to say.

"So is she!" Jo laughed as she headed towards the bathroom.

"Samantha, what do you mean?"

"I don't know Charlie. Darrin is great and I really love him. Sometimes I think he's the one I'm going to spend the rest of my life with. But then Rose…..Rose is amazing! She's sweet, considerate and patient. We have so much in common and I think I'm falling for her. The way I feel when I'm with her is just…I can't describe it."

"Plus she's eating that pussy up!" Jo returned.

I turned to say something smart but Sam stopped me with her next statement.

"We haven't had any kind of sex. We've only kissed."

I glanced at Jo and her mouth was on the floor.

"Oh….so does Darrin know about her?" I asked.

"No, but she knows about him. She's never pressured me to do anything. When I stay over at her house we usually fall asleep on the couch talking or watching tv. I've never even slept in her bed."

"Pick up your jaw Jo," I said without looking back at her.

"You mean to tell me you two have been 'friends' for months now and she's not tried to get in your panties at all? Oh, she's got a piece on the side."

"Or she's a grown-ass woman Josephine! Not everything is about sex. We have a deeper connection."

"Sure pal."

"Jo." I said softly.

"Why do you always take her side?" Jo demanded.

This evening was not going how I planned.

"She does not always take my side. Why are you always a jerk?! Why don't you grow up?!"

"Guys please." I tried again but it was pointless. Now they were both standing up and yelling at each other. I sat back just watching it unfold. Maybe they just needed to get it out. After about five minutes Jo said she was leaving and headed towards the kitchen to grab her phone.

"I have cancer."

Jo stopped dead in her tracks and Samantha sat down hard on the floor. It was complete silence for a few minutes as the deadly word hung in the air.

"The doctors caught it early. I've had a few chemo treatments already. I should be getting another scan next month after my last treatment. They're pretty positive that I'll make a full recovery." I went over my prepared speech almost mechanically. It was all true but I was still terrified. When I looked up, Jo was standing next to Sam holding her hand. This was one of the rare moments I could see the resemblance between them. They were fraternal twins and while you could tell they were related, most people never guess they are twins.

"Someone please say something." I started crying and they both rushed to me and sat onto the couch next to me. A twin on either side.

"Why didn't you tell us? We would have been there with you." Samantha asked quietly.

"I didn't want to worry you two unless it was necessary. Michael has been with me for every single appointment. The chemo hasn't been so bad. It's a new treatment. I didn't even lose my hair!"

Here I was during my crisis trying to comfort them. It's how it always was. Our parents were killed in a car accident when I was 23, the twins were 16. I was in my last year of college when it happened but I immediately took a leave of absence and came home to take care of them. Even though our aunt Renee stepped in and they could have gone to live with her and our cousin Alex, I didn't want them to have to change schools right before their junior year. So I petitioned the court to let me be their guardian. Ever since then, I've been even more overprotective than a normal big sister.

Sam sensed what I was doing and wrapped her arms around my shoulders and pulled me close to her for a hug. "Charlie, it's okay to need us. We're here for you just like you've always been there for us."

I relaxed into the hug and broke down. I didn't realize how much I had been pretending to be okay for everyone else when really I was terrified and tired. I laid in Samantha's arms crying while Jo laid her head on me and hugged me from behind. I don't know how long we sat like that but I eventually was all cried out and surprisingly I felt better than I had since I'd found out about the cancer.

"I'm sorry I didn't tell you two earlier but I promise to include you from now on. For the record, Michael was against me keeping this from you from the beginning…"

"Danielle?" Sam asked with eyebrows raised.

"No, we didn't tell Dani. The doctors really do think we caught it early enough so we didn't want to upset her unless it was necessary." Just the thought of my little girl almost made me tear up again. She was 10 and my whole world. I couldn't imagine what it would do to her if something were to happen to me. I was an adult when our mom was killed, but it still rocked me to my core. It's a pain that I still felt every day.

"That's a good idea. No need to worry her because you're going to be fine." Sam smiled at me.

I realized Jo was unusually quiet. I repositioned so that I was facing her. "You okay?"

"Of course I'm okay. You know I'm always good." She smiled but it didn't quite reach her eyes. Jo took it really hard when our parents were killed. She had gotten into an argument with our dad earlier that day. The guilt from whatever was said between them and not being able to fix it ate at her. She rebelled against me for a while before finally getting it together. While in college, she bought two-night clubs with her friends (against my wishes) that were doing really well. Then when she graduated she decided to go into the Air Force. I was super proud of her.

I reached up to touch her cheek but Jo wasn't one for all this gushy stuff, as she would call it. She grabbed my hand and kissed it before clearing her throat and standing. She kissed me on the forehead and squeezed Samantha's shoulder as she walked into the kitchen. A few seconds later, I heard the door to the patio open and shut.

"Just give her a minute. You know how Jo gets." Sam offered. I nodded my head.

"How long are you in town?"

"Well I was supposed to leave Sunday but I was thinking about staying an extra couple of days. I could use a little getaway. Would that be okay?" I asked hopeful as the thought just occurred to me.

"Of course it's okay! I would love to have you around longer. I miss you so much, sis!" Sam hugged me again.

"Okay, I'll call Michael in the morning. I'm sure they could get along without me for a few days. So, you gonna tell me more about what caused this 'friendship' with Dimples?" And just like that, I slid back into big sis mode. It's what was comfortable for all of us.

Sam started telling me about her wet dreams and how her and Rose met at one of Jo's clubs. We were laughing about something when Jo slid back into the living room. She refilled everyone's wine glass and sat on the floor near me. She jumped into the conversation as if she had been there all along. Adding that she tried to fire Rose for dating Sam but when she ran her background check and found out she was a detective she decided against it. I thought that news would spark another argument but Samantha just rolled her eyes at Jo.

We had a good time catching up until we were fighting to keep our eyes open. Me and Sam trudged up the stairs to go to sleep. Jo volunteered to crash in Sam's office so I could take the guest room. My eyes were closed before my head hit the pillow. It felt good to be under the same roof as the twins, even if it was only for a couple of nights. Just what I needed- twin therapy, I smiled as I drifted into a deep sleep.

ROSE

———◁✦▷———

"What's wrong baby?" I answered Sam's call just before five a.m.

"Charlie has cancer." She cried quietly into the phone.

"Oh no. I'm so sorry. You want me to come over?" I was already halfway out the bed.

"No, I'm okay. It just caught me by surprise. She's always been the strong one and I can't imagine her being anything other than that. I don't know what I'd do if I lost her."

"I'm on the way." I hung up before she could object again.

Twenty minutes later I was at her front door. She had texted me that she was getting in the shower and the front door was unlocked. I let myself in and made my way upstairs to her bedroom. She was already asleep when I climbed into bed with her. She stirred when she felt me get in the bed and rolled over to lay on my chest. I wrapped my arms around her and whispered, "I love you" before falling asleep.

I woke up a little after nine and Samantha was still knocked out. I eased out of bed and pulled my sweats on. Closing the bedroom door quietly, I jogged downstairs and ran into Jo in the living room.

"I was going to grab breakfast for these two. Want to ride?" She asked without batting an eye.

"Sure. I guess great minds think alike. I was going to get coffee."

We walked in silence to Samantha's car. Once we pulled into traffic, Jo cleared her throat a couple of times, like she wanted to say something so I went first.

"I know you love your sister and you want to protect her but you should know that you're not the only one."

She raised an eyebrow and glanced at me, "Okay, are you saying you love Samantha?"

"I do and I would never hurt her or let anything bad happen to her."

"I can appreciate that but what if you are the bad thing?"

"Meaning what exactly?"

"I don't think Sam really knows what she wants right now. It's easy to get caught up in…"

"Look, technically Samantha and I are just friends. I've been here for her while she tries to figure out what she wants. I haven't done anything to influence her decision. We enjoy spending time together and if you're concerned about someone getting hurt it's probably gonna be me. So, you can save whatever speech you have prepared."

Jo opened her mouth to say something and then closed it again. She nodded her head and finally said, "I think I'll just mind my business."

I nodded back and we both got out of the car to go into the store. We grabbed stuff to make breakfast, coffee, and mimosas. Jo's mood was lighter since our talk so I decided to roll with it. Maybe she really will back off and mind her own business. She said Erica would be joining us at the condo for breakfast too so we made sure we had enough food for everybody.

When we got back it was still quiet so we started cooking. I was surprised that Jo seemed to know her way around the kitchen. We were about halfway done when I looked up and saw Samantha leaning against the doorframe smiling and watching us.

"Well good morning sleeping beauty." I pulled out a stool at the counter and poured her a cup of coffee.

"I thought I was dreaming about you being in my bed this morning." She smiled happily at me.

"So you're dreaming about me now?" I asked. I thought I heard Jo snicker behind me but then the doorbell rang so she darted out of the kitchen to answer it. Samantha looked a little flustered but she hid her face in her coffee mug.

"Hey, y'all! It smells good in here!" Erica came around the corner holding Jo's hand.

"Girl they cooking breakfast," Samantha said to Erica.

"Here babe." Jo handed Erica a champagne flute with a mimosa.

"Okay then!" Erica giggled.

"Damn what smells so good?" Charlie was the last one to enter the kitchen.

"We decided to make you ladies breakfast," I answered. "Coffee or mimosa?"

"Coffee now and mimosa once the food is done. Thank you." She said as she took the mug from me.

"Am I late to the party?" I heard a male voice before seeing a face. All the color drained from Samantha's face and the way everyone else in the room froze, I could only assume I was about to meet Darrin. I backed away from the island where Samantha was sitting.

"Charlie! When did you get here?" He exclaimed as he turned the corner and saw Charlie. She smiled before turning to face him.

"Hey Darrin. I got in last night to surprise Samantha." They embraced.

"It's good to see you. I hope we get to catch up while you're here." He responded.

Samantha hadn't moved yet. It was like she was frozen in time.

"What's up Erica? Jo?" He nodded at them both and looked questioningly at me but turned to Samantha first.

"There's my girl. Hey, luv." He leaned down and kissed her passionately.

I felt like someone had just punched me in the gut.

"Hey, babe. What are you doing here?" Samantha muttered as she pulled away from him.

"We had plans for breakfast, remember?" He turned towards me.

"Hi. I'm Darrin, Samantha's boyfriend." He extended his hand to me. I stared at it for a second debating if I should punch him in the face for touching my girl. Then I remembered she wasn't mine, she was his. I glanced over at Samantha, she put her head down.

"Uhh....Darrin this is Rose. She works at one of the clubs." Jo spoke up since the cat had my tongue.

I finally put my hand out to shake his, "Darrin, good to finally meet you. I've heard a lot about you."

"Really?" He smiled and turned back to Samantha, "well since you're about to have breakfast. You want to go do something after?"

"I think I'm going to head out guys. I have some errands to run." I forced myself to turn away from their interaction. "I'll hit you up later Jo." I dabbed her and headed out of the kitchen. I had to get out of there before I lost it.

"See ya later!" I heard Charlie or maybe Erica yell after me. I grabbed my car key fob off the living room table and yelled, "okay" behind me. I was focused on making it to the door.

I got off the elevator and hit the unlock button. Just before I got to my car I heard Samantha call my name. I stopped for a second but then kept going without turning around.

"Rose please!" She ran to catch up to me and stood in front of me.

"What Samantha?"

"I didn't know he was coming. I would never put you in that position."

"It's fine." I clenched and unclenched my jaw and my fist.

"It's not fine. You're upset and I'm sorry."

"Samantha I knew what I was getting into when we started…..this is but I didn't expect to start falling for you. And I didn't expect to ever have to see the two of you together. Watching him kiss you and put his hands on you, I wanted to knock his head off. He was just a name before now but this isn't right. I don't want to play a part in hurting or deceiving someone and I damn sure don't want to feel how I feel right now. I need to step back from…..from you. Maybe us spending all this time together isn't helping you make a decision about anything. It's not fair to me to just wait for you when you don't even know what you want." I could feel myself getting more and more angry but I refused to cry. She was though.

"I never asked you to wait for me and I didn't intend for any of this to happen. I'm falling for you too. I don't want anyone to get hurt and I don't want you to step back. Rose please just give me a little more time. Please don't say goodbye. I need you." She stepped closer to me and reached to put her hand on my arm and I stepped back out of reach.

I didn't know what to say. I didn't think she was falling for me or that she would admit it if she was.

"Sam….I...I"

"Just promise me we can talk later? That when I call you, you'll answer? That's all I want from you right now." She stepped towards me again, invading my personal space with her scent.

"I can't promise anything right now." I stepped around her and got in my car. I heard her say something else but I turned up my music and burnt rubber out of the garage. I looked in my rear-view mirror and she was still standing there crying. It took everything in me not to get out of the car and run back to her. To sweep her up in my arms and hug her but I couldn't do that. I needed to figure out what I wanted before she called me because I knew I was going to pick up that phone no matter what I had just said.

I drove around for about an hour trying to clear my head before I finally pulled up at my best friend Ryan's house. I hadn't seen my godson in a little while and I figured a three-year-old would be a great distraction. Ryan's wife, Sara, answered the door and smiled when she saw it was me.

"Rose! Ryan, didn't tell me you were coming by. Come in!" She stepped back to let me in after giving me a hug.

"Hey sis. I was in the area so I decided to stop by. I didn't call Ryan. Is it a bad time?" I had my hands in my pockets and shuffled my feet instead of accepting her silent welcome into their home.

"Don't be silly. Ryan just went to the grocery store to grab something to throw on the grill. We did a coin toss to see who got to stay home with the monster and I lost." Sara giggled as she joked about my godson Carter.

"He can't be that bad." I laughed and stepped over the threshold into the house.

"I'll let you be the judge of that. Carter, Titi Rose is here!"

I immediately heard what sounded like a herd of small, but loud, elephants stampeding downstairs all while yelling "Titi Rose!!"

Next I saw the cutest, curly headed, chocolate kid ever. As soon as he was close enough he launched himself into my arms and squeezed my neck. This is exactly what I needed, I thought to myself as I squeezed him back. The hug only lasted about 30 seconds before he was squirming to get down. As soon as his feet touched the floor, he was pulling me into his playroom to show me his new basketball game. I looked back at Sara who was laughing as she followed us to the back of the house.

"Can I get you a drink or something?"

"No thanks, I'm good. I'll hang out with him if you want to relax."

"Oh I am definitely disappearing into my room for a while. Ryan should be back soon. Tell him to let me know when dinner is ready!" She was gone from the doorway so quickly that I had to laugh. I played basketball with Carter on his pint-sized basketball hoop until I heard Ryan come in. Sara must have told him I was there because he didn't seem surprised to see me in the playroom, holding Carter so he could dunk the basketball.

"What's good bro?" He dapped and hugged me.

"Daddy, titi Rose is not a boy." Carter corrected Ryan.

"You're right Carter. Can I borrow your titi Rose?"

"Okay. I gonna play cars by myself. Titi Rose can you watch a movie with me before you leave?"

"Of course buddy. Just pick something good." I ruffled his curls before following Ryan into the kitchen where he already had the groceries on the counter.

"Sara said she's in your room and to let her know when dinner will be done." I sat at the counter and accepted the beer Ryan handed me.

"I know, she texted me that you were here so grab another steak and do not disturb her unless it's for food or wine." Ryan rolled his eyes and laughed. "What's been up with you? Sorry I had to cancel our basketball game last week. Carter had t-ball registration and it took longer than I thought it would."

"It's all good. We still on for next Saturday?" I asked sipping my Corona.

"Yeah, he plays in the morning so we should be good for our regular time. If you want to come to his game, it's in the same area."

"You know I'll be there."

"Cool. Let's go outside so I can put the food on the grill."

I walked ahead of Ryan to open the patio door since he was carrying two pans with steak, potatoes and corn on the cob. I leaned against the gate that enclosed their pool and stared off into space. My mind was still racing trying to figure out my next move with Samantha. She had texted me while I was playing with Carter, that she was sorry and if we could meet later to talk. I just saw the message and was debating on responding when Ryan joined me at the gate.

"So who is she?" He asked.

I put my head down before answering. Apparently, my acting wasn't as good as I thought.

"Her name is Samantha."

"I'm listening….."

I spent the next forty-five minutes filling him in on everything from how we met up to a couple of hours ago and everything in between. He didn't speak until I was finished.

"Rose, you know I love you but you gotta stop doing this to yourself. There's gotta be some women that are actually gay out there! Sorry that wasn't cool but I hate seeing you get hurt from dealing with these confused females."

"I know, I know. I didn't plan on this. I thought maybe I'd smash, satisfy her curiosity and dip but our connection is so deep. I'm not even tripping on the fact that we haven't had sex or anything like that. I just love being around her. I don't know what to do Ry."

Ryan sighed and rubbed his hand over his face. We'd been friends for about 15 years. The closest thing I'd ever had to a sibling.

"I know it seems the same but she's not Gloria. Plus, I'm not the same. I refuse to let anyone take me back to that dark place. I promise." I looked him in the eyes so he could see how serious I was.

"Okay from what you've told me she does not sound like she is intentionally set on hurting you. However, that is what is happening and what will continue to happen if she doesn't make a choice. If you care for her the way you seem to genuinely care for her, let her go.....Let me finish. I mean stop making yourself so readily available for her every time she calls. Maybe you should date other people. Like you said, it's not really fair for you to sit around waiting for her while she's got a whole relationship on the side. I'm not saying cut her off completely but a little time apart and with someone else might provide you both with some clarity."

"That's not what I want though. I want her. I want a chance at happiness like everyone else."

"She can't be your happiness if she belongs to someone else. That's not God's plan and you know that."

"Alright where's my dinner and my wine?!" Sara came out on the patio just in time to end this conversation. Ryan looked like he wanted to say more but he turned to face his wife instead.

"I don't know what you're talking about, woman. I only cooked enough for me and Rose." He held his palms out and shrugged his shoulders.

"Then I guess I'll be eating yours then."

We sat out on the patio until Carter held me to my word to go watch Toy Story 4. About halfway through the movie he fell asleep so I carried him to his room and tucked him into his bed. Sara and Ryan were in the kitchen cleaning up after dinner. When I came into the room, Ryan had his arms around her waist and was whispering in her ear while she stood at the sink washing dishes. This scene was heartbreaking to me as it symbolized everything I was missing.

I cleared the lump out of my throat. "I'm gonna head out guys. It's getting late."

"Aww okay hon. Are you coming to church tomorrow?" Sara asked as she came around the counter to kiss me on the cheek and hug me.

"Yeah, I think so."

"I'll walk you out." Ryan said coming up behind Sara.

"That's okay. I don't want to disturb you guys any more than I already have. I'll see you in the morning." I backed out of the kitchen and to the front door as quickly as I could without running. There was no way I wanted to finish the conversation from earlier. Ryan had made himself very clear and I had made up my mind.

JOSEPHINE

"Well this is awkward," Erica leaned over and whispered in my ear. We were sitting at the table eating breakfast. Charlie was talking to Darrin and Sam was completely zoned out. Every once in a while, Darrin would say something to her and she would chime in just enough to satisfy him.

When Sam ran after Rose, Erica and Charlie kept Darrin talking and distracted so he wouldn't notice what was going on around him. I just stood back. I saw the look of hurt and anger in Rose's eyes before she left. I knew that look all too well. To think it was only a couple hours ago that Rose said she was probably going to be the one to get hurt and then low and behold she did. Regardless of how much I disliked the situation, I must admit I liked Rose and I actually thought she was good for Sam. Who knows what's going to happen with them now.

Charlie got up from the table to answer a call on her cell. Darrin turned to Samantha, "you okay baby? You look kind of pale." He reached out to feel Sam's forehead.

"I feel like maybe I'm coming down with something." She mumbled.

"Maybe you had too much to drink last night?" Erica offered.

"Do you need me to go get some medicine from the store? We don't have to go out today. We can stay in and watch Lifetime movies all day. I'll go pick up medicine, and snacks." Darrin said with a smile while rubbing his thumb over Samantha's finger.

"That sounds great….."

"Why do I sense a but coming? Samantha I've barely seen you the last couple weeks." He almost sounded pitiful.

"What do you mean? We go out every Sunday."

"Not lately and what about the other days during the week? Something feels different and I was looking forward to seeing you today."

Darrin was doing his best to talk quietly but since we were all at the table together that was pointless. Me and Erica were faking a conversation so it wouldn't seem like we were listening but we totally were.

"I'm sorry you feel that way but other than busting my ass to make sure my firm got that account, nothing has changed. I apologize if I haven't been able to spend as much time with you as you've grown accustomed to but my career is important too. I was looking forward to seeing you but I didn't know Charlie was going to be here. I haven't seen my sister in months and I would like to spend some time with her without feeling guilty."

Samantha on the other hand was not trying to talk quietly. I could see Darrin grit his teeth and draw into himself a little. In the two plus years they had been dating, my twin had never said anything negative about him. He really was a good guy and I honestly felt bad for him too.

"It wasn't my intention to make you feel guilty Samantha. I know you haven't seen Charlie in awhile. Why don't you call me later and we can set something up for next week?" He pushed back from the table and kissed Sam on the forehead. "I love you. Erica. Jo." He nodded to us and walked out of the room. I heard him saying goodbye to Charlie and then the front door closed.

Charlie walked back into the kitchen looking puzzled. "Why did Darrin leave so suddenly?" She asked.

"Yeah Samantha, why did he leave so suddenly? Aren't you going to run after him like you did Rose? Or is that behavior saved only for your side chick?"

"Fuck you Jo! Cause you're so fucking perfect!"

"No fuck you Sam! You're screwing over two really decent people all because you're being greedy! Grow the fuck up and stop playing with peoples emotions!"

"Don't confuse me with the bitch you were stupid enough to fall for. Get off your high horse…."

"That's enough dammit!" Charlie yelled so loud Erica jumped. "I don't know what the hell has gotten into you two but I'm sick of it. Since when do you talk to each other like this?"

"I don't have time for this shit. I'm a grown ass…" Samantha stood up from the table.

"If you don't sit your grown ass down." It had been a long time since I had seen Charlie like this which means we must really be acting out of pocket. Sam sat down real quick though.

"No one is leaving until I say so. Erica, you are free to go or stay. It's up to you."

"Umm as much as I would love to stay and take part in this sistervention, I think I'm going to head out." Erica kissed me on the cheek, "call me later." She got up, walked around the table, hugged and kissed Charlie and Samantha before heading to the front door.

And then there were three. I sat back in my chair, smirked and clasped my hands behind my head. This should be fun. I thought to myself.

"Who wants to go first?" Charlie asked, looking between the two of us.

DARRIN

————◁◆▷————

Sitting in my car I tried to figure out if it was just my imagination that something seemed off with me and Samantha's relationship lately. I knew she had been busy with work lately but was that really it? Or am I being paranoid? Maybe I need to fast forward my plans to propose on her birthday? I mean I already had the ring so why not? She could be pulling away because she's tired of being a girlfriend. I understand that because I know I'm ready to move on to the next level in our relationship. I want to marry her, buy a house and start a family. Just then I saw Erica enter the garage and head towards her car. Perfect timing!

"Erica! Hey you got a second?" I jumped out of my coupe.

"Darrin. You scared me. What's up?"

"I need your help with something."

"Sure. What ya need?"

"Planning Samantha's proposal." I grinned from ear to ear. Erica on the other hand did not seem as happy as I thought she would be.

"Oh! I didn't know you guys were..uh..at..uh" she stuttered.

"Well we HAVE been together for almost 3 years now. I think it's time. Don't you?" I was puzzled at her response.

"Yeah….it's just…you know Samantha's really focused about her career. Are you sure now is the right time?"

"Well us getting married doesn't have to interfere with her career…."

"You're right. I'm just being selfish about losing my girls' weekends. I'm going to run some errands right now but why don't we get together in a couple days and we can come up with a killer proposal plan?"

"Okay great! Thanks!" I gave her a quick hug and turned to walk back towards my car. "Erica I hope you know it's not my intention for our relationship to interfere with your friendship. I know you two are like sisters and I don't want to change that. You will still have your girls' weekends."

"Thanks Darrin, that means a lot to me. We'll talk soon." She smiled and walked away.

I got in my car smiling as well. As soon as I backed out of my parking spot I hit the phone button on my dashboard, "call mom," I said out loud. After a few rings, my mother's voice came on the line.

"Hey ma. Guess what?"

SAMANTHA

------◁✦▷------

After the emotionally draining morning and afternoon I'd gone through, the only thing I wanted to do was talk to Rose. I'd called and texted a couple times already but no answer. Our 'sistervention' as Erica had called it went surprisingly well considering how angry Charlie was when we started. I hadn't realized my love life was a trigger for Jo and everything she went through with Monica. On one hand, it's my life and I shouldn't care what anyone says but on the other hand, it wasn't my intention to hurt anyone. As of right now, I'd hurt several of the people closest to me.

After talking to my sisters, I know I have to make a decision and soon but I'm no closer to figuring out my feelings than I was when I first started this journey months ago. I looked at the clock on my nightstand and realized it was after midnight but I was not physically tired, just mentally exhausted. I got off the bed and put on some black leggings and a red long sleeve t-shirt. My slides were by the front door with my keys. Maybe a drive will help clear my mind. I almost wish I had gone to hang out with Charlie and Jo just to take my mind off missing Rose. I got in my car with no real direction but somehow I knew where I was going.

Sitting in Rose's driveway, I debated if this was the right decision or would she just cloud my judgment more or worse, reject me. Either way, I had to do something. I got out of the car and called her phone on my way to the front door. I wasn't expecting her to answer this time any more than she had the last several times I had called but surprise -

"Hello". Hearing her voice actually stopped me in my tracks before I reached the door. I was even more certain this was the right decision.

"Hey" I responded barely above a whisper.

"Samantha, I don't want to do this right now. I'll call you tomorrow…."

"Even after I drove all this way to see you?"

"Huh? You're here? Why would you do that without calling first?" I could hear her moving around and then I saw a light come on in her bedroom.

"Rose please….I need…."

The front door opened and she was standing there with her long black hair framing her face. She had on a tank top and sweatpants. I couldn't tell if she was happy to see me or not and that broke my heart. She stood back and held the door open, inviting me in.

"Look, Samantha..I..." she started to say once she closed the door but as soon as she turned around to face me I stopped her with a kiss. She initially didn't kiss me back but after a few seconds she wrapped her arms around my waist and pulled me closer to her. "Sam..."

"Rose, I need you. Make love to me." I had my head down afraid for her to see how afraid I was.....afraid she would turn me away....afraid she wouldn't.

She gently pulled my face up and stared into my eyes. I could see the hurt and confusion in her eyes that matched the mix of emotions in mine. Just when I thought she was going to turn me away, she bent down and kissed me so soft and sensual it almost felt like goodbye. But then she parted my lips with her tongue and slid it in my mouth. I moaned low and stood on my tippy toes, in an attempt to deepen the kiss. She broke away, grabbed my hand and led me towards the stairs.

Once we were inside her bedroom, I gently pushed her to sit on the bed and took off my shirt, followed by my leggings. I stood in front of her completely nude for the first time. She got up and walked towards me.

"Are you sure?" She asked but I had lost my voice along with my inhibitions, so I just nodded, "damn you're so beautiful." The way she looked at my body made me blush.

She walked backwards to the bed and like a magnet my body followed. When she sat down she kissed my stomach and caressed my hips. I straddled her lap and she immediately flicked her tongue over my nipple sending a chill down my spine. She alternated between both breasts licking and sucking them both equally. I moaned and yearned for more. I wanted to feel and taste her body too. Running my hands through her hair and down her back, I pulled her mouth away from my breasts for a kiss. She stopped me by sliding me off her lap onto the bed next to her. While I slid backwards closer to the headboard, she stood up and disrobed before climbing on the bed with me. I took that moment to take charge of how I wanted this to go. I straddled her again and this time flicked my tongue across her left nipple, then alternated between licking and sucking both breasts like she had done mine. She moaned and closed her eyes. I started kissing my way lower towards her stomach and then her thighs.

She sat up a little, "Samantha you don't have to do that. This is your first time so I….."

I stopped her mid-sentence as I licked her clit timidly at first to determine if I liked the taste then more aggressively once I realized she tasted good! Rose collapsed back on the pillow muttering curse words. I remembered reading somewhere about "writing" the alphabet with your tongue so I tried that in between softly sucking her clit. Judging by the way she was moaning and cursing I think I was doing it right not to mention the amount of her juices that were all over my chin. After some time, Rose was grabbing my head and calling my name then she suddenly stopped. I couldn't help but smile as I looked up at my sexy, sweet, macho detective laying there satisfied from my handiwork. She caught the look of pride on my face and pulled me up to her.

"Oh you think you did something?" She chuckled while kissing me and tasting herself which turned me on even more.

"I mean..." I laughed and shrugged my shoulders.

"Oh okay then," she laughed and flipped me off her onto my back.

"Where you going?!" I yelled as she jumped off the bed and went into her walk-in closet. She came back a few seconds later with a black toiletry bag. I raised my eyebrows and my body up to see what was inside.

"Uh-uh no peeking." She said so I laid back down.

Then she was laying on her side right next to me again.

"What's in the ba…." Before I could finish, something with a strong vibration was placed between my legs.

"Shhhh," was her response before getting on top of me and kissing me deeply.

I opened my legs more so that she was laying between them and holding onto whatever was giving me this immense pleasure.

"I love you Samantha."

"Fuuuuuck!!!"

I awoke the next morning alone in Rose's bed. I rolled over to look for my phone to call her and found a note on the nightstand.

Hey beautiful,

I had a training session that I couldn't get out of. I'll be back soon...with breakfast.

I love you.

I laid back and held the note to my chest. There was that word again. Rose had said I love you twice now and I didn't know how to take it. Part of me felt like coming here last night was a mistake yet part of me was elated. However, all of me was even more confused than ever. I knew I was falling for Rose. Who was I kidding, I knew I was in love with her. The issue I was having was deciding if I was only considering Darrin out of obligation or did I still see a future with him. Sleeping with Rose last night only made my vision cloudier. I decided to freshen up before Rose got back with breakfast.

I walked back into the bedroom just as she was walking in carrying coffee and a bag from Einstein's Bagels.

"Good morning." I smiled at her as I watched her eyes trail over my naked body.

"It is now." She answered seductively.

Instead of getting back in the bed I walked into her closet and grabbed one of her t-shirts to put on. Otherwise there wouldn't be any talking this morning. As I enter the bedroom, she's stripping out of her gym clothes.

"Damn." I mumbled to myself. Or so I thought.

"Don't get excited. I'm going to shower." She laughed when she saw my face. On her way to the bathroom she stopped and kissed me. "I got your favorite but I also got two blueberry bagels because somehow mine always seems to disappear quickly when you are around."

"I have no idea what you are talking about." I dramatically rolled my eyes.

I sat up in the bed munching on one of the blueberry bagels and sipping coffee. Pure heaven. I must have had my eyes closed savoring the moment until I heard a soft chuckle from the other side of the bed. I opened my eyes to Rose smiling at me.

"Enjoying your breakfast, I see."

I smiled and nodded since I had a mouthful of bagel.

She chuckled again and reached for the bag to get her bagel. Then instead of joining me on the bed she sat down in one of the recliner chairs in her bedroom's sitting area.

I cocked my head to the side and raised my eyebrow questioning her distance.

"I think we should talk and I think better when I'm not next to you."

I nodded in agreement and sipped my coffee. We sat in silence for a couple minutes, each lost in our own thoughts. Rose was the first to break the silence.

"Samantha, as amazing as last night was, I don't want to be naive or assume anything. I know what it meant to me but I kinda would like to hear from you…."

Here we go, the moment of truth. I still had no idea what to say or who to choose.

Who the hell is calling me from the hospital?

ERICA

"Hey baby," I smiled into the phone.

"Hey babe. Can I come over?"

Ooh I loved when her voice had that morning raspiness to it.

"Of course. I was expecting you to come last night after y'all talked. Was it that bad?"

"Nah it was actually pretty decent. I'll tell you about it when I get there. You need anything?"

"Just you." I answered seductively.

"On the way."

I hopped out of bed and went into my bathroom to get ready. After brushing my teeth and washing my face, I pulled my honey blonde curls out of their pineapple ponytail. I gave my hair a breather for about two weeks in between getting it braided. I added a little product to my hair and smiled at my reflection. I decided to keep on my boy shorts and tank top because I knew it turned Jo on but I didn't want to seem too desperate so I waited for her downstairs instead. I could pretend to be watching TV, I laughed to myself as I grabbed a big soft blanket and tossed it on the couch before heading into the kitchen to make a smoothie. Just as I was pouring two glasses, I heard her motorcycle pull up and a few minutes later her key in the front door. When she walked into the kitchen and smiled, I got butterflies.

"Just in time. I made you a smoothie." I walked towards her with the glass.

"You always know how to take care of me." She took the glass, put it on the counter, wrapped her arms around my waist and buried her face in my neck.

"You okay babe?" I asked after a couple minutes once she didn't let go or try to grab my butt like she normally does. She didn't verbally respond, just nodded her head. We stood that way in silence for a few minutes until she broke free and kissed me on the lips. Then she smiled and picked up her smoothie before sitting on one of my barstools.

"What was that all about?"

"I just missed my girl that's all," she winked at me.

"Mmhmm, okay. Anyway, so tell me about y'all sistervention." I laughed at the name I had made up. Jo didn't laugh, she rolled her eyes instead.

"Not much to say really. I finally got Sam to see things from a different perspective other than her own. I told her that seeing her do the same thing to someone else what Monica did to me was kind of painful to watch." Jo shrugged her shoulders.

"It's not really the same thing though."

"Why isn't it?"

"Well, Samantha isn't sleeping with Rose and she definitely isn't doing it in the bed she shares with Darrin." As soon as the words left my mouth, I regretted them.

"That's a nice way to sum it up."

"Jo, I didn't mean to say it that way."

"But you meant to say it? Regardless of if Sam is actually sleeping with Rose or not, you do realize she's still cheating on Darrin?"

"I don't think so. She's dating…"

"You can't fucking date someone else while in a committed relationship. They don't have an open relationship, Erica."

"I know that but…."

"But what? I'm trying to see where your head is at with this. So, you're saying it's okay for me or you to go out and date someone else right now?"

"Not necessarily but I also didn't know we were in a committed relationship."

"Then what are we doing?"

"I thought we were dating."

"Dating or fucking? Who else are you dating?"

"Do you even know the difference? And you know I'm not dating anyone else. I don't even get down like that. What's wrong with you?"

"Nothing is wrong with me but you sound stupid as hell right now."

"Okay what you not gonna do is continue to disrespect me in my house. So you can either calm the hell down or get the hell out."

"You right, I'm sorry. But if this is how you really feel about what Sam has going on then that makes me question…..everything. There's more than one type of cheating. Monica was emotionally cheating on me way before she was physically. And that's exactly what my sister is doing. To think you agree with that. I thought we were building something. Shit it's bad enough you kept your college girlfriend a secret from…."

"Whoa. First off, I think you've talked enough so why don't you just be quiet for a minute. I didn't say I agreed with Samantha's decisions but I am trying to be supportive to her while she tries to figure out some shit. I am also aware that there is more than one way to cheat. However, Josephine, I am not Monica and I am not Samantha. So, I would suggest you stop comparing me to either of them. I am a grown ass woman and I know who I want. Now up until about fifteen minutes ago I was pretty sure that I wanted you but don't make me question that because you can't get past someone else's indiscretions. DO NOT interrupt me. Second off, my college girlfriend was not a secret. I did not expect for you to share all of your past relationships nor did I think I was required to. I have never intentionally kept anything from you so if it's something you want to know just ask me dammit. However, not right now because I am officially done with this conversation. Maybe you should go home and take a cold shower or a hot bath or something to calm your nerves and I'll call you later." With that I slammed my smoothie glass on the counter and stormed into the living room, flopped onto the couch and picked up the remote. I was slightly holding my breath waiting to hear her leave.

After what seemed like an eternity but was actually more like five minutes, I heard the barstool scrape across the floor. She walked into the living room with her hands in her pockets. She stood in the doorway shuffling her feet for a couple of seconds waiting to see if I would acknowledge her which I did not.

She cleared her throat, "Erica? I'm sorry."

"Save it Jo." I didn't even look away from the TV.

She walked to the couch and kneeled on the floor next to me.

"Baby, I mean it. I know you aren't Sam or Monica. The hurt that I felt..I wouldn't wish that on my worst enemy."

I softened my posture and turned towards her when I heard her voice crack a little. "Jo…."

"Please let me finish."

I nodded my head.

"That was a really low point for me. I didn't think I would ever give my heart to anyone again. Then, that night we went out and I sensed there could be a chance to be with the woman of my dreams. But I was, hell I am, still scared. The way I feel about you is different than anyone else….."

"Because I'm different." I blurted out.

"Woman hush," she laughed, "but yeah you are different. I'm also different now that I'm with you. I won't let anyone come in between what we have. So, I really am sorry for taking all of that out on you. You didn't deserve that. Forgive me?"

"Jo, in case you forgot, I was around during that time. I saw how she hurt you. I was on the phone with Samantha many a night debating on driving around looking for Monica to beat her ass. Don't laugh, I'm serious. I would never hurt you in that way. I told you when we first started dating, that I would tell you if I was having second thoughts about us and I meant that. I'll forgive you on one condition."

"I'll never compare you to anyone other than you."

"Oh I know you won't make that mistake again but that's not my condition."

"Okay what is it then?"

"We make this official. That way there's no question on if we're just dating…"

"Or just fucking?"

"Whatever." I rolled my eyes at her. "So….that's my condition. Take it or leave it."

"I'll take it cause I can't leave you. Especially since we just survived our first fight and you are sexy as hell when you're mad. Can I pick a fight once a week?"

"I wish you would. Now come sit down so I can get back to my show."

"Only show you getting back to is our regularly scheduled morning program if I hadn't screwed up this morning."

"I don't know what you're talking about. My plans were for us to watch a movie and chill."

"In those boy shorts?" She asked as she pulled my blanket back.

"Yep. Now cut it out. I'm serious." She stood up and pulled off her t-shirt, leaving only a sports bra and revealing her six-pack abs. Next she kicked off her boots and stepped out of her jeans. She was wearing a pair of the boxer shorts I bought her. Ugh, her body was so incredible. "I don't know why you're stripping. You're not getting any."

She climbed onto the couch and straddled my legs. She bent down to give me a kiss or so I assumed. Instead, she whispered, "so your not turned on right now?"

"Not in the least bit." I whispered back.

"So, you not wet right now?"

"No....."

"I thought you said you'd never intentionally keep anything from me?" The whole time she was questioning me, she was trailing one hand down my stomach and with the last question her hand was in my boy shorts where she could clearly tell my last answer was a lie.

"Do you want me to stop?" She asked, staring into my eyes.

I shook my head no since I wasn't sure if I could actually answer her.

"One more question. Rough and fast or gentle and slow?"

"Both."

She grinned as she slid a finger inside me, "that's my girl."

JOSEPHINE

---◁✦▷---

A couple hours later, I woke up spooning Erica on her couch. I was starving but I didn't want to wake her. She looked so peaceful with her hair wild all over, almost like a halo. I slid from behind her as gentle as I could and grabbed my cell phone out of my jeans. A quick bathroom break later and I was in the kitchen rummaging around for snacks. I found some cheese, crackers, grapes and wine. Where's the real snacks? This would have to do for now I thought as I put everything on a tray with 2 wine glasses. I laid a blanket out on the living room floor, with the tray and attempted to wake my love from her slumber. A couple of kisses was all it took before she was up.

"You hungry?" I asked as she stretched and yawned.

"Starving. What time is it?"

"Almost four."

"Dang, we was sleep for a minute."

"Nah baby we wasn't sleep that whole time." I laughed.

"Oh…yeah." She blushed a little and smiled.

"I got something for us to munch on. Come sit on the floor."

"You always trying to woo me with a picnic," she laughed playfully.

"I think I've done a pretty good job with and without the picnic."

"You right." She answered while popping a grape in her mouth.

"You want me to put on a movie?" I reached over and smoothed her curls a little.

"No, put on some music instead. Let's talk."

"Uh oh."

"Girl put on my Jade Novah playlist and hush."

"Oh no Jade means it must be serious," I joked, grabbing the remote for the Smart TV from under the couch while she rolled her eyes at my comment.

"Anyway, you asked about my girlfriend from college."

"Babe you don't have to talk about that. I didn't mean what I said earlier."

"No, it's okay. Like I said it's not a secret just not something I talk about too much. Very few people even know about her. I met her at a Kappa party my Sophomore year. We hit it off immediately - as friends. We hung out damn near every day. I had no idea the rumors that were going around that she was a lesbian and I was her newest conquest. Well until Samantha told me. I immediately defended Cheri and even said to Sam, so what if I was. I then confronted Cheri about her sexuality, accused her of wanting more and not being honest about her intentions towards me. She admitted that she was gay and she was interested in me as more than a friend. At first, I was angry but then I must admit I was a little curious. I finally agreed to let her kiss and fondle me but I wouldn't touch her. It was really selfish of me."

Erica paused for a minute to sip some wine and I could tell this was not easy for her to talk about it.

"So, one night we both got really tore up at a party. I came on to her, wanting her to go farther than we had. About ten minutes into her giving me oral sex, I started to freak out. I accused her of taking advantage of me and I called her all types of horrible names. She ran from my dorm room in tears and wrapped her car around a telephone pole. Her blood alcohol level was more than double the limit. They say she died instantly. No one ever knew the extent of our 'relationship'. Most people, including your sister, thought we were an actual couple. Other than my therapist, you are the first person I have ever told."

"I...I don't know what to say." I was actually speechless. What do you say to something like that?

"You don't have to say anything. I've spent a lot of money on therapy and I've done a lot of work on myself to heal from all the guilt I felt, that I still feel for her death. A part of me knows it's not my fault but a part of me feels if I hadn't caused her to run out that night she would still be alive. I told you this because I want you to know how much I mean it when I say I won't string you along. I would never do that because I've seen the repercussions firsthand. I hope this doesn't make you look at me any different. It was a long time ago and I am most definitely not that person anymore."

"I don't look at you any differently other than admiration for you persevering through all of that. I can't imagine what that must have been like for you. Thank you for trusting me with that piece of you. I'll protect it the same way I promise to protect the rest. Come here." I gently pulled Erica to me and hugged her tight, kissing her on the forehead.

"Why don't you go take a shower while I clean all this up and we get some real food?" I asked.

"That's a good idea babe." She kissed me on the cheek and got up off the floor. She stopped at the doorway. "Jo?"

"Yes luv?" I looked up from my cleaning.

"Thank you." She didn't wait for my answer before she turned and jogged up the stairs.

CHARLOTTE

"I miss and love you too baby girl. Talk to you later. Put your dad back on the phone. I'm glad to hear you guys are surviving without me. I was thinking, why don't you two come up for the weekend? I know Dani would love to see her aunties and I miss you."

"Or you could come home Charlotte. You have a chemo session this week. You can't keep trying to fix all of the twins' problems baby." Michael said in his usual calm demeanor.

"I know but I haven't seen them in awhile and things are such a mess. I emailed my doctor and I can miss this week without any setbacks to my treatment. I just need a little more time. Please don't fight me on this Michael."

"We've been together long enough for me to know what battles are worth fighting and anything that involves your sisters is a no no. Me and Danielle will be there Thursday night and we are leaving together as a family on Tuesday. Deal?"

"Yes my luv. Thank you. I'll see you in a couple of days." I blew a kiss into the phone before hanging up.

I didn't know if I would actually be able to 'fix' anything in the next few days but I damn sure was going to try.

"Hey, Samantha. I was just about to…..wait calm down. What hospital? Okay, I'll try to call Jo again . I'm on the way. Love you sis."

Michael talking about coming home but this shit is like a damn soap opera. Sam has her girlfriend dropping her off to the hospital to check on her boyfriend. What the hell?

"Josephine, where are you? Call me back ASAP! Better yet meet me at Emory. Darrin was in a car accident. Sam's a nervous wreck."

Less than fifteen minutes later, I was parked and rushing towards the entrance. I almost crashed right into Rose coming out.

"Rose! What happened?" I exclaimed as soon as I saw her.

"The hospital called Samantha as Darrin's emergency contact. She was so shook up that I couldn't let her drive but I'm sorry I couldn't sit up there with her. I waited a few minutes but I knew you would be here soon. His mom is on the way too and that would be even more awkward. I didn't want to leave her but I just couldn't…."

"It's okay. Thank you for at least bringing her. Rose it's clear that you care about my sister and I wish things weren't the way they are right now. You're a good person and I pray things work out however God sees fit for you." I could tell she was really struggling with her decision not to stay with Sam. I gave her a hug and promised I would update her later before running off to find Sam.

I found her in the Emergency Department waiting room. Her eyes were red and swollen. When she saw me, a fresh flow of tears slid down her cheeks.

"Charlie!" She cried out as I grabbed hold of her.

"Shhhh, it's okay, I'm here, I'm here." I wanted to ask her if she had gotten any news but I was afraid of her answer.

"Ms. Riley?" A nurse called out.

"Here!" I answered for Samantha as we stood up together to get the update.

"Mr. Mathis is out of surgery. We were able to stop the internal bleeding and he's stable. Once he is out of recovery in a couple hours you will be allowed to go visit."

"Thank you." Samantha stood there like a zombie so I answered for her.

"Sam, he's going to be okay."

"This is all my fault Charlie. God is punishing me for sleeping with Rose."

"When did that happen? Never mind it doesn't matter. God is not punishing you and Darrin is okay. You heard the nurse."

"I know but…."

"No but's. Get yourself together before his mom gets here."

"Okay. Were you able to reach Jo?"

"No, I left her a message. I'll call Erica."

"I tried her too. Hopefully they'll call back soon."

"I'm sure she will luv. Why don't you go to the bathroom and wash your face? I'll wait here in case Mrs. Mathis comes." She nodded and exited the waiting room.

I took my phone out of my back pocket to try Jo again and saw a text from her and Rose.

```
Jo: Shit sis, my phone was on
silent! Me and Erica will be at the
hospital in a minute.
```

Thank God. As much as Samantha was glad that I was here, I knew having her twin here is what she really needed. I checked the message from Rose next.

```
Rose: I was able to find Jo, she
was with Erica. They should be
there soon. I hope everything's
okay.
```

Wow, I could definitely see what attracted my little sister to Rose. After all of this, she still went out of her way to make sure Samantha was taken care of. I don't know if this accident was enough to pull her back to Darrin or not but I see why she's torn. A few minutes later, Mrs. Mathis, Jo and Erica all came into the waiting room together. I gave them the update from the nurse while we waited for Sam to come back. She returned fully composed, until she saw everyone waiting. She didn't fall apart but she did get emotional again greeting everyone. I could see the relief on her face when she saw Jo. That's the bond I knew them to have. Eventually, someone from the hospital escorted us to a waiting room on the floor where Darrin's room was located.

Once in the new waiting room, it was just us. I called Michael to let him know what happened and to assure him they didn't need to come sooner. I shot Rose a text to let her know Samantha seemed to be doing okay. Darrin's mother was on the phone with some of their family updating them. Erica went to grab coffee for everyone. I don't know what it is about coffee and hospital waiting rooms. Seeing Sam curled up in a chair with Jo protectively sitting close by reminded me so much of the night our parents were killed. Sitting in the hospital waiting room just like this one, only to find out the doctors weren't able to save them. They were together for 30 years and died within 30 minutes of each other, all due to some kid, barely older than the twins were at the time, texting while driving. Three lives taken, two families heartbroken and a lifetime of pain for everyone involved.

About an hour into the wait, I could feel my anxiety creeping in and my chest getting tight. I shot my hubby a quick text.

```
Charlie: Hey, on second thought if
you're able to get away from work
then you guys coming earlier isn't
a half bad idea.
```

I'd barely hit send before he responded.

```
Michael: We're already on the way.
See you in a couple hours. Stay
strong my, luv.
```

Overcome with a range of emotions, from gratitude to grief to love, I quietly slipped out of the waiting room to the bathroom so no one could see me cry. When I came out of the stall, both twins were waiting for me. Either they sensed my emotions or they were feeling the same way. Either way I was grateful they came to check on me. No one said a word, we just stood there in the bathroom, holding onto each other.

SAMANTHA

The sun felt good against my skin as I lay on the beach in Bermuda. This was just what I needed after the last three months. My life changed so quickly it was almost like a dream. After Darrin's accident, I knew I had to make a decision about who I wanted to be with and I can't say that I'm 100% secure in my choice but it was the right thing to do. That should count for something, right?

"You coming to get in the water baby?" Darrin appeared dripping wet and blocking my sun. Even though I can't say that I minded the view, he was cute, wearing only swim trunks.

"I can't get my hair wet before the wedding tomorrow. But afterwards, absolutely." I smiled up at him with my hand shading my eyes so I could get a better look at him.

"Okay, I guess. I'm gonna go play a game of volleyball with the guys. You need anything?"

"I got everything I need, baby. Go have fun, love you," I blew him a kiss and he winked before jogging off down the beach, leaving me alone with my thoughts.

The day I broke it off with Rose was about as painful as when I found out about Darrin's accident. I had been by his side almost every minute while he was in the hospital. She'd only text me once but I found out later that she had been checking on me through Jo and Charlie, to be respectful and give me my space. When Charlie had to go back home, I got really sad. Having her around made everything seem like it was going to be okay. Darrin's mom, Ms. Sarah, sensed my energy one day when she came to check in. She made me go home and get some proper rest. I was ordered not to come back for at least 36 hours. I was actually relieved but without the distraction of being the doting girlfriend, I realized how much I missed Rose and how this was all so unfair to her. After I showered and made myself presentable, I called and asked her to come over.

The hug she gave me when she got there almost made me change my mind. It had been about two and a half weeks since I last saw her. That was the longest we'd been apart in the seven to eight months we'd known each other.

"I missed you," she mumbled into my hair.

"I missed you too."

She accepted the beer I offered her before we sat outside on the patio. We sat in silence for a few minutes, enjoying the peace of the night air. She finally asked how Darrin was doing. I let her know he was doing much better and expecting to be released from the hospital next week. She nodded her head and took another swig of her beer.

"Okay, Samantha, out with it." She said quietly.

"What do you mean?"

"You didn't call me over to 'break up' with me?" She did air quotes with her fingers.

"Is it breaking up if we aren't technically together?" I responded.

"Don't bullshit me please. The least you can do is just give it to me straight. You thought he was dying and it made you realize that you are still in love with him and I was just a phase. Does that about sum it up?" Her voice was flat but she wasn't angry.

"Kind of but not quite." I responded with my head down as tears escaped from my eyes.

"What did I miss?"

"You...were not a phase. And yes I realized I love him but I am in love with you."

"Then why are you crying Sam?"

"Because I can't do this anymore. It's not fair to you or him!"

"Now you want to talk about fair? Was it fair when you came to my house in the middle of the night to fuck?"

"Rose please....I don't want to end like this..."

"Why? Because you still want to be friends? I've been your friend for a while now and I don't think that's a friendship I care to continue."

"Rose, I'm sorry...." I was damn near bawling at this point.

"Answer this question, Samantha. You claim you're in love with me but you're going to go live happily ever after with him?"

"It's the respectable thing to do."

"Because we all know how respectable you are?"

"That's not fair! I've always been honest with you. You knew what this was from our very first conversation. Don't try to play the victim now."

"You're right. And this....this right here is my karma." Her voice cracked and I realized she had tears in her eyes. "Goodbye Samantha." She got up from the table and bent down to kiss me on the forehead. "I would have given you the world if only you could have given me your heart."

After she went in the house and I was sure she had left, I went inside, drank three shots and cried myself to sleep on the couch. I was certain I had just said goodbye to the love of my life.

I hadn't heard from Rose since although her and Jo ended up being friends and I know they hung out occasionally. Which thoroughly pissed me off. In the meantime, I focused on my relationship with Darrin. Things between us are really good and I'm grateful that he's almost back to his old self physically. While physically, I was doing my best not to compare him sexually to the one night Rose and I shared. Easier said than done but I've gotten pretty good at faking it. Sex with Darrin had gotten better but he still wasn't her.

I looked at the time and realized I needed to find the rest of the wedding party and get ready for the bachelorette party.

DARRIN

"Bro, you sure about this? It wasn't that long ago when you said Samantha was reading hot and cold….shit more cold than hot. Now you want to marry her?"

Robert and I were sitting on the balcony of my suite, having a drink and watching the waves of the ocean roll in and out. We had about an hour before we needed to start getting ready for the ceremony. I was trying to keep my cool as he was questioning my decision to marry Samantha because I knew it was out of love but he was starting to get on my nerves. I took a deep breath and another sip of my drink before getting ready to respond.

"Don't get me wrong D, I love Samantha. She's like a little sister to me but I don't want you to rush into something that you'll regret later."

"I appreciate you looking out, Rob but I know what I'm doing. Samantha's been by my side everyday since my accident. We're stronger now than ever. Hell she practically lives with me and you know she was strong in her belief that we wouldn't live together before marriage. That alone shows me how committed to us she is. This is it man. It's time." I said as resolutely as I could without coming across as aggressive as I wanted to.

"Alright man, say no more. I just want my best man to be happy. I tell you what though if I catch flak from Kelly about you proposing on our wedding weekend then I'm beating yo ass."

"You couldn't beat my ass in college and you damn sure can't now. Let's go get yo pretty boy ass ready for your big day and I'll try not to look better than you." We both laughed and shook hands before heading inside to get dressed.

ERICA

"Babe what's a U-Haul lesbian?" I asked Jo while we were cuddled up on her couch.

"A lesbian who moves in with her partner really quick, like the second date. Where'd you hear that?"

"At the nail salon. I overheard two girls talking about one of their friends and they said she was acting like a typical U-Haul lesbian."

"Oh." She moved from where she was laying on my lap and sat up.

"Relax. I'm not asking if we can move together. I know we're not ready for that step yet." I laughed at the nervous look on her face.

"Oh good." I could see her shoulders relax.

"Girl you know you wish we lived together so you could have this anytime you wanted." I rubbed my hands over my body and laughed.

"I can already have this anytime I want." She winked and rubbed her hands over my hips. She leaned in for a kiss but then her phone rang with Samantha's ringtone.

"If she's calling while on vacation it must be important." I said when it looked like she was going to let it go to voicemail.

Jo groaned and reached over to grab her cellphone off the coffee table.

"What's up twin?" She answered on speakerphone.

"I'm engaged!" Samantha screamed into the phone.

"Oh my gosh bestie! Congrats!" I screamed back. I was glad she didn't FaceTime Jo because her face was not exactly happy.

"That's what's up sis. I'm happy for you." Her tone was just above dry but it didn't seem like Samantha caught it.

"Thank you guys! I gotta call Charlie next. See you in a couple days, love ya!" She hung up before we could even reply.

"Baby, you knew this was coming. I told you he asked me to help plan it." I rubbed Jo's arm after she tossed her phone back on the coffee table.

"I know but I was hoping she wouldn't say yes."

"What made you think that? Has she said something about Rose?"

"Not at all. She acts like she never existed and I know she misses her. I could respect it more if Sam chose Darrin because she loved him but not because she feels obligated or something."

"I agree but that's her choice. We can't do anything about that. How is Rose? Talked to her lately?"

"Yeah I played ball with her and Ryan last weekend. She's okay I guess. You know she took the breakup really hard. She still asks about Sam every now and then. I tried to convince her to start seeing someone but she said she's not ready yet."

"I don't blame her. After a heartbreak like that you don't want to rush into another situation. That's how people get hurt. Did she ever get back to you about coming to the birthday party?"

"True. Nah she said she wasn't sure if she was ready to be in the same place as Sam and Darrin."

"Poor Rose. I think Samantha was happier with her. Just the way she talked about her and lit up in her presence. As much as she loves Darrin, I don't think it's the same. But like I said it's not our business so stay out of it." I got up to go find a snack in the kitchen.

"Where you going?"

"I'm hungry!" I yelled from the kitchen.

"You always hungry! Don't be just walking around my house like you live here. We ain't U-Hauled yet!" I could hear the smile in her voice even though I couldn't see her face. I came out of the kitchen eating an ice cream sandwich.

"Yet? Who said I want to U-Haul? Ain't no shacking up. If you want all this on a regular basis you gonna have to put a ring on it." I did the Beyonce, Single Ladies dance with my hand.

"Oh really? I didn't realize that was something you wanted."

"Yeah. Is that a problem?" I leaned against the wall and crossed my arms. Hoping this was not going to turn into a debate….or worse.

Jo didn't answer right away, I guess she was thinking.

"No, not at all." She grinned really big, "But if you drip that ice cream on my rug then that's going to be a problem." She got up off the couch and walked towards me. "When the time is right and we're both ready, I would love for us to get married and have kids - if you want them. All those things that people in love do. Is that the answer you were looking for?"

I nodded my head, surprised at what she had said but elated to know we felt the same way.

"Good. Now come on and let's go get yo hungry ass some real food."

"Let me see the ring!!" I exclaimed as soon as Samantha made her way to the table where I was waiting for her.

She flashed her hand and a huge smile to match the huge rock on her ring finger.

"It's beautiful!" We hugged before sitting down.

"I ordered you a white wine spritzer. I hope that's okay."

"That's perfect!"

"So how was the rest of your trip? Did you guys set a date yet?"

"The trip was perfect. It got better after the wedding though."

"Because of the proposal?"

"No, because we got to spend more time alone. I adore Robert but Kelly, not so much."

"Really? I thought you two were cool?"

"We were but you remember she was rude to…....She's just a little more uppity than I care for that's all. So what have you been up to this last week?"

Just then the waitress came with our drinks and asked if we were ready to order. I took the moment to think about what Samantha didn't say. It must have been Rose that Kelly was rude to. That would explain the sudden shift in the conversation.

"Not much. I held the office down while you were out. Jo and I decided we're getting married and having kids."

"Wait...what? I was only gone a week, right?"

I laughed at Samantha's reaction. "Not right now but we talked and it is something we both want in the future."

"That's great Erica! We'll officially be sisters!"

"I know! Oh we hung out with Rose and her best friend Ryan this weekend. Her godson is absolutely adorable." I paused to gauge Samantha's reaction to hearing Rose's name.

"Oh…..why?" She asked calmly.

"Why what?"

"I'm not with Rose anymore so why are you guys hanging out with her?"

"You know her and Jo are still cool. They actually play ball together. I just decided to tag along because I didn't have anything else to do."

"I wish you two wouldn't do that. It just makes things awkward."

"Awkward for who? It didn't seem awkward to me." I laughed her off and sipped my drink.

"I just…..don't like it and I don't want to hear about her. I'm happy with Darrin and that's that!"

"Ohhhkaaay….. well now that we've cleared all that up. Did you get an outfit for the party next weekend?" I decided to change the subject because clearly, I was right on how she really feels about the whole situation. She's not over Rose.

Samantha took a couple deep breaths to gain her composure before answering, "No. I was going to ask you if you wanted to go to Lennox with me tomorrow to find something."

"Oooh that's a good idea. I think I'm supposed to be meeting Jo for lunch but I'll see if she wants to do dinner instead."

"Okay, let me know."

The waitress arrived with our food and we spent the rest of the evening talking about her and Jo's party.

CHARLOTTE

———⊰♦⊱———

"Dani, I know you want to come with us to see your aunties for their birthday but me and your dad could really use a little vacation. I thought you'd be excited about staying the weekend at Janelle's house?"

"If I'm such a great kid then why do you need a vacation from me?" My daughter pouted while I put her hair into a French braid before church.

"Hey you're not only a great kid you are the best kid. We don't need a vacation from you, we just want to spend some time together. I'll make a deal with you. When we get home from church, I will call your titi Sam and see if you can go visit her for a week when school lets out."

"Just me? Why can't I stay with titi Jo too?"

"Yes, just you. And because last time you stayed with titi Jo she let you drink ketchup."

Danielle laughed and rolled her eyes, "Mom! That's when I was five. I don't even like ketchup anymore."

"I wouldn't either if I drank it." I laughed with her. "I'm sure we can work it out where you can spend time with both of your aunties. Deal?"

"Deal." She popped up as soon as I put the rubber band on the braid. "Thanks mommy!"

"We're leaving in 20 minutes!" I yelled after her as she ran out of my bedroom.

"I know!" She yelled back.

I stood in my closet trying to figure out what I was wearing to church. I didn't hear Michael enter the closet so he startled me when he came up behind me and wrapped his arms around me. I leaned into him while he snuggled my neck.

"Is she still pouting about not coming with us to Atlanta?" He asked.

"No, I told her she could go visit without us when school gets out next month. I'll call Sam when we get home later to work out the details."

"Good idea babe. I put the breakfast dishes in the dishwasher and the salmon is marinating to go on the grill later. If we don't get out of here in the next 10 minutes we won't be able to sit where we usually sit. You know that section fills up fast." He kissed me on the cheek before letting me go.

"Thanks honey and okay I'm just gonna throw on a dress."

"Woman. When do you ever 'just throw on' anything?"

"You got jokes. I'll be ready in a couple minutes. Go check on your daughter and make sure she's not trying to wear jeans."

"Okay. We'll meet you downstairs."

"Hey sis. What's up?" Samantha answered on the 2nd ring.

"Hey your favorite niece wants to know if she can come stay with you for a week when school lets out next month? I figured maybe she can spend a couple days with you and a couple days with Jo. What do you think?"

"That would be great! Let me check my work schedule and see when will be a good time to take a couple days. Can I let you know when you come to town this weekend for the party?"

"That's cool. She's not happy with us for not bringing her to the party so this was my bribe to get her to stop pouting."

Samantha laughed, "I understand sis and I would love to spend some time with my baby.'

"Good! Are you sure you don't need me to come early to help decorate?"

"I'm sure, Jo hired a party planner and a caterer to come in and handle everything. We met with them weeks ago to go over what we wanted. We don't have to do anything but show up, look good and have a good time. That goes for you too!"

"Okay, okay, okay," I laughed. "What time are you guys supposed to arrive?"

"I'm not sure that we're arriving together anymore. We kind of had words the other day soooo…"

"Seriously? For what now?"

"Erica told me that they've been hanging out with Rose and I don't like it. So I told Jo she shouldn't be hanging out with my ex."

"I can only guess how well that went." I sighed and rubbed my forehead.

"She told me that it was selfish of me to tell her who she can be friends with and just because I broke up with Rose didn't mean she had to."

I knew Samantha was waiting for me to take her side and tell her that Jo was wrong but I didn't know if I could this time.

"Well Sam I don't know if I'm on your side on this one. Rose didn't do anything to hurt you that would cause Jo not to like her. They also work together so it's quite natural that they would keep some sort of friendship. Why does it bother you so much that they are hanging out?"

"I just don't want to hear about or see her."

"Is that because you still care about her?"

"No….I'm happy with my choice to be with Darrin."

"I know. You tell me every time we talk."

"Because it's true. I wish everyone would stop questioning that. I made a choice and I just need everyone to accept and respect that."

"Okay, no one is questioning your choice or disrespecting it. It wouldn't matter to me who you chose to be with as long as they treat you right and you're happy. You do know that right?"

Silence…..

"Samantha? Tell me you know that."

"I just want mom and dad to be proud of me." She whispered into the phone with tears in her voice.

"Oh Sam. Mom and dad would be so proud of you. You are strong, educated, independent and successful. I promise you they would say the same thing to you….just be happy. Life is too short to be anything but that baby sister."

"Charlie, I gotta go. I'm meeting Erica at the mall to find an outfit for the party and I want to stop and see Darrin first. See you in a couple days. Love you." She hung up before I could reply.

I groaned loudly just as Michael came in from outside with the salmon and vegetables for dinner.

"What's wrong babe?" He put the food in the oven warmer and joined me on the couch.

"I just got off the phone with Samantha."

"Okay. Did she say no to letting Danielle come spend some time with her?"

"Oh no. She was really excited about that idea."

"Oh good that will make our leaving this weekend easier. So what's up then?"

"She told me that her and Jo had an argument because Jo is still hanging out with Rose. Apparently, Sam thinks that's disrespectful and after that conversation I can't help but think Sam is still in love with her. I think she chose to be with Darrin for all the wrong reasons."

"Charlotte don't start. This weekend is supposed to be a vacation for us. Not a chance for you to play Iyanla Vanzant and fix your sister's lives."

"Well that was extreme." I started to get up from the couch but he placed a hand on my arm to stop me.

"Wait. That came out harsher than I intended. I know you are worried about the twins and you want to make sure they are taken care of but you have to let them be adults. Let them live their lives and make their own choices. I want to spend some time with my gorgeous, cancer free wife this weekend. Don't make me play second to the drama with your sisters."

His words were so sincere. My husband had been by my side through so much. He was there when my parents died, he understood when I left school to take care of the twins, supported and encouraged me to finish my degree later, cried with me through three miscarriages and now we can add beating cancer to the list. He was such an amazing husband and father to our daughter. He deserved to have my undivided attention this weekend.

"You're absolutely right baby. We deserve some time to celebrate and reconnect. I promise to not partake in any twin drama this weekend. I'm going to make some rice and bread for dinner. Do you want a beer?" I could tell he was expecting a bigger fight out of me. He sat there stunned for a minute and I couldn't help but laugh.

"Sure, I'll take a beer." He finally managed to get out. I gave him a peck on the lips, handed him the remote and a cold beer before heading back into the kitchen. I'll just have to do my damage control before we get to Atlanta so that I don't ruin my weekend with Michael.

```
Charlie: Hey Rose! I hear you're on
the   fence   about   coming   to   the
twins'   birthday   party.   Well   I
expect you to have hopped off the
```

```
fence and to pull up. Can't wait to
see you, no excuses. Smooches luv.
```

That should get the ball rolling.

JOSEPHINE

"I'm just sick of her thinking everything has to be her way. She's too damn old to be a spoiled brat."

"So you'd cancel your party and lose thousands of dollars just to spite Samantha?"

Erica and I were having dinner after her and Sam's shopping trip.

"I don't give a damn about the money. It's to prove a point Erica."

"I understand that baby but can you prove a point another time? Please? It's your 30th birthday. You deserve this party and you deserve to see me in the outfit I bought for the after party."

"What after party? I don't want to go through with the main damn party. Why would I have an after party? Oh…..." I caught the look on Erica's face and realized she didn't mean an actual after party. "Don't try to threaten me with a good time and your body."

"Is it working?" Erica laughed.

I rolled my eyes in response.

"Seriously babe, what's it going to take to ensure you have a good time for YOUR day?"

"Nothing. I almost wish I hadn't agreed to celebrate with Sam. Every birthday we've celebrated together ends up being all about her." I clenched my teeth just thinking about all the birthdays ruined because of my twin.

"I'm sorry. I didn't know that. Well I'm going to do my best to make sure this is a positive and memorable birthday for you."

I couldn't help but smile, "I like the sound of that and I'm gonna hold you to it."

"You can. Are you coming back to my place tonight?"

"Babe you know I have to go in early on Mondays."

Erica immediately started pouting.

"So why don't you come stay at my place instead?"

"I guess that can be arranged. I just need to go home and pack a bag." She smiled.

"You have clothes at my house already."

"Are you sure?"

"Yes babe. You have a dress, a pantsuit, workout clothes, pajamas and underwear. What else do you need?"

"Oh. Is that too much? I don't want to crowd you."

"No. It only makes sense that you have things at my house and vice versa as much time as we spend with each other. Don't you agree?"

"I do but I wanted to make sure it wasn't too much for you."

"I can't get enough of you so no it's not too much. You ready to go?"

"Yeah baby. I'm ready."

"Babe, is Sam in the office today?"

"No, she's out today and tomorrow to get ready for the party. What's up?"

"The party planner is at the club waiting for her. She scheduled a walk through with them. She's an hour late and won't answer the damn phone! I swear she…."

"Okay no worries. The club is close by, I'll just go meet them."

"See this is exactly what I meant about her being selfish and ruining shit."

"Hey I told you, I got you baby. Tell them I'm on the way and I'll be there in 10 minutes. Do you want me to call you when I get there?"

"No that's okay. I trust your judgment."

"Okay. See you after work?"

"Yeah babe. I'm staying a little late so I'll come by your place when I get off."

"K," she blew a kiss into the phone and hung up.

I was beyond aggravated with my twin but I sighed with relief knowing that Erica was going to take care of everything. Samantha better have a good ass excuse for being MIA. About 30 minutes later, my phone dinged with a text notification.

```
Erica: Hey baby. The place looks
great! You're going to love it. I'm
actually going home instead of back
to the office and I ordered from
```

> your favorite Thai place for dinner. See you later.

I smiled at my phone and before I could text back my phone dinged with another text.

> Sam: I completely forgot about the walk through and scheduled myself a massage for the same time! I haven't been able to reach the party planner but I'm headed to the club now. Sorry!

I ignored the text from my sister, not my problem. I sent a quick text to Erica instead.

> Jo: Thank you. I really appreciate you handling that. I'll see you in a little while.

I packed up my stuff and decided to go meet her for dinner.

"Good night Captain Riley."

"Good night Lieutenant Smith."

I walked outside to a beautiful day. I'm glad I decided to leave early. I think I'm gonna drop my car off home and ride my bike to Erica's. Maybe I can convince her to take a ride with me tonight. I've been working on getting her on the back of my bike for months now. I looked down to see who was calling as I pushed the keyless start in my truck. Once I saw it was Sam, I turned my phone off, turned up my music and pulled out of my parking spot.

"Yes but Charlie, why do I always have to be the bigger person? It's not my fault that she double booked things. I've planned and basically paid for the whole party like it's not my birthday too! She had one job and she couldn't even do that. I am **not** apologizing this time. Okay…..Love you too. I'll see you tonight. " I hung up my cell phone and rolled my eyes.

Rose laughed, "I see Charlie is still doing her big sister thang."

"Is she?! Man I'm so sick of everyone placating Samantha and her bullshit. Anyway, speaking of big sister thangs…Charlie told me she was expecting to see you tonight at the party? Does she know something I don't?"

Rose drank some of her beer before answering, "she sent me a threatening text last week. And as scared as I am of Charlie…..and trust me I am scared of her," she laughed, "I'm still unsure about coming. I just don't know about being in the same space as your sister and Darrin. I mean I would love to come celebrate with you but….."

"I feel you but the club is huge! I have the whole second floor blocked off as just our VIP section. You'll barely be breathing the same air as them. Just come for about an hour."

"Okay."

"Okay?"

"Yeah, okay. I'll be there."

"Bet! You'll have a good time!"

We finished our beers before I went to pick up Erica from the hair salon.

ROSE

I can't believe I was 'bullied' into coming to this party. Why did I feel like I was going to regret this decision? Nonetheless here I was, dressed up and looking sexy if I do say so myself and headed to make more poor decisions. Seems like my life has been full of those. I was even regretting asking Sierra to be my date tonight. I knew she liked me and I was not at all interested but I didn't want to look pitiful by myself. I pulled up to the valet and debated about pulling off but just then I got a text from Sierra saying she was inside waiting by the bar. Damn, too late to turn back now. Why didn't I just bring Ryan? I hopped out and the valet recognized me.

"What's good Rose? I was wondering when you were gonna show up. The boss said to keep your car close. Is that okay?"

"Yeah, that's cool. Thanks man." That made me even more nervous. I guess Jo was expecting me to make a run for it early.

I nodded at the bouncer as he opened the door and then headed to the bar to find Sierra. She wasn't hard to find in a bright yellow bodycon dress that hugged her curves. Damn she was fine, she just wasn't Sam.

"Don't you look good."

She smiled when she saw it was me.

"Mmm you too. I didn't think you could look better than you do when you're sweating in the gym."

I laughed at her compliment. She had been one of my personal trainer clients. After she asked me out and I told her I don't date my clients, she fired me. I finally admitted to her that I had just gotten out of a relationship and I wasn't ready to date yet. She said she was okay with us just being friends and agreed to come hang out with me tonight.

We headed upstairs to the VIP section. When we reached the top, the first person I spotted was Charlie. She jumped up from the couch and ran across the floor to give me the biggest hug.

"Rose! I'm so happy to see you! How have you been? You look great." She asked when she released me from her grip. I couldn't help but smile at her warmth and energy.

"I've been good. I'm happy to see you and you look amazing as always. I love the new haircut!"

"Thank you!" She looked over my shoulder and smiled at Sierra.

"Sorry, this is my friend Sierra. Sierra this is Charlie. She's sister to the guests of honor."

"Nice to meet you." Sierra reached her hand out but Charlie gave her a hug instead.

"You too! Come meet my Michael." Before I could answer she was darting back across the room to her husband. We followed behind her but got stopped by Jo.

"Bro! You made it!" She hugged me almost as tight as Charlie had.

"Yeah I'm here."

"I'm so glad. Let me get you a drink." She turned to signal a waitress.

"I'm not drinking tonight Jo. You can get something for my friend Sierra though. What you want to drink?"

Jo turned back around, "Not drinking? You gotta do at least one shot with me. It's my birthday. Hey, nice to meet you sweetheart. Two shots of Peach Crown and whatever she's drinking." Jo said to the waitress when she appeared.

"You too and happy birthday. I'll take a Ciroc and pineapple. I'm going to find a bathroom," Sierra whispered in my ear. I nodded in acknowledgment.

As soon as she was out of earshot, Jo said, "Sam's gonna be pissed you brought a date. She's already mad because Darrin isn't here yet."

"She's not my date. Just a friend but why should Sam care? Why isn't Darrin here?"

"She'll care because she's still in love with you but shit don't tell her I said that. Take this shot with me so I can go find my cup."

Rather than argue with her I took the shot and when she turned her back to look for the vanishing cup, I picked up her shot and threw it back too. "I don't think you need your cup Jo. Where's Erica?" Jo was already tipsy and didn't even realize I took both shots. She walked away saying she would be right back. I went to find Charlie so she could introduce me to Michael but instead ran into Samantha and Erica coming off the dance floor.

"Hey Rose! Have you seen Jo?"

"Yeah, she was looking for her cup."

"Again? Ugh thanks." She walked off to find Jo.

"Hey" I said as nonchalantly as I could to Samantha even though inside my heart, stomach and everything else was doing jumping jacks.

"Hey" she answered back, trying not to make eye contact.

"Damn…..you look…..gorgeous. Happy Birthday."

"Thank you. I should go check…"

"There you are! I was looking everywhere for you. Hi, I'm Sierra." Talk about horrible timing. Samantha looked Sierra up and down and then looked at me.

Samantha rolled her eyes and then stormed off.

I turned to face Sierra and plastered a fake smile on my face.

"Ouch. That must be HER."

"Uhh yeah, that's the other birthday girl. I think she was running to the bathroom." I laughed nervously. "I see you got your drink."

"Yep. You wanna dance?"

Behind her I could see Samantha and Jo arguing. "Good idea." I grabbed her hand and led her to the dance floor. I could still see Samantha from where we were. She took two shots back-to-back and I groaned inward. That wasn't a good idea considering she got tipsy after a couple glasses of wine.

"You okay?" Sierra asked.

"Huh? Yeah, I'm good. Sorry. Are you having fun?" I smiled at her, trying hard not to look at Samantha as she pouted in our direction.

"I am now." Sierra smiled back and put her arms around my neck.

I stopped a waitress carrying shots and took another one - so much for not drinking and making bad decisions.

"Me too." I gave her my undivided attention for the next 5 or 6 songs. We danced so hard I realized the saying "dance your cares away" was a literal saying.

"I'm gonna go get some water. You want anything?" I asked Sierra.

"No, I'm good. I'm gonna stay out here for a bit."

"Okay, I'll come find you after I catch my breath." I laughed.

I grabbed a bottle of water off one of the tables and leaned on the arm of the couch while drinking. I could see Jo and Erica dancing close by and Charlie and Michael were on one of the other couches talking. I realized I still hadn't met him but first a bathroom break.

The women's and men's bathrooms were on opposite sides of the room. I hated that there was only one stall but since we were separated from the rest of the club there was no line in the dark corner.

When I came out of the bathroom, Samantha was sitting on the arm of one of the couches in the bathroom lobby where there was normally an attendant. She had her arms crossed, she was clearly angry and absolutely beautiful.

"How could you bring a date to my birthday party?"

"Are you stalking me?" I joked, "and she's not my date. We're just friends. Not that it's any of your business."

"No, I'm not stalking you. And it's my birthday so it's my business."

"That's not how this works baby." I laughed again.

"Don't call me that."

"Sorry, force of habit. Look Samantha, I'm here because your sisters both asked me to be here. I didn't want to disappoint them and if you have a problem with that then you'll have to take that up with one of them."

"I did and Jo called me selfish. Do you think I'm selfish?"

"I don't…"

"I miss you."

"Sam, don't….."

She uncrossed her arms to push her hair behind her ear and her ring caught the light.

"You're engaged?!"

She stopped and put her hand behind her, almost in embarrassment.

"I can explain."

"What's there to explain? You're going to marry Darrin?"

"I don't know."

"You don't know? Samantha, you're wearing his ring. That's usually what that means."

"I know what it means but…."

"But what?"

"I hate when you cut me off! Damn can you just let me talk?!"

I opened my mouth to say something and closed it again.

"Yes I am engaged but I am not sure if he is the one. These last few months without you have been miserable. I think about you all the time, when I'm awake, when I'm asleep, other times when I definitely should not be. I miss you but I don't know how to be with you. I'm not brave enough to be with you. I know you probably hate me and I don't blame you but I just wanted you to know how I feel…… Now you can talk."

I sighed loudly, "Samantha, I don't hate you, I could never hate you but I can't stay on this emotional roller coaster with you. If I can't have all of you then I won't settle for half. I deserve more."

"You're right. You do deserve more. I just wish I could give it to you."

"Yeah, me too." I started to walk away but she stopped me.

"So how have you been? I see you're dating. She's pretty."

I sighed and rubbed my hand across my face, "I'm not dating. I'm not ready for anything like that. Sierra was one of my clients."

"Then why would you bring her here?"

I paused before answering, deciding how honest I wanted to be, "because I didn't want to show up here alone and pitiful while you're living happily ever after with your fiancé." That came out sounding more bitter than I expected it to but nonetheless it was how I felt.

"Rose….I'm sorry."

"Don't apologize. You should go after what you want." I was starting to feel the 3 shots that I had earlier so I sat on the couch near Samantha. "You should be with who adds to your happiness Sam. I can't be mad if that person isn't me. I love you enough to be at peace with that."

"What if Darrin isn't that person?"

"Then I don't know what to tell you."

"Did you get me a gift?"

"Did I get you a what? Shit I barely want to be here." I blurted out and laughed at myself for being so honest.

"Damn it's like that?"

I nodded my response.

"I'm sure you have something you can give me?"

"Like what?"

"A kiss?"

"I don't think that's a good idea." She came in closer to me. Her perfume circled around me, suffocating my already slightly intoxicated senses.

"Please? For old times' sake?"

"Sam, I'm not playing these games with you." It was too late, she was almost straddling my lap and before I could attempt another protest, she was kissing me, sliding her tongue into my mouth. My reflexes instantly pulled her on top of me as I wrapped my arms around her waist. Damn I missed her, missed this. She was my kryptonite and as much as I wanted to I couldn't resist her. She ran her hands through my hair, deepening the kiss and I had one hand on the back of her neck while my other hand was pulling up her dress.

"Tell me you still love me." I demanded.

"I still love you." She said in between kisses.

"She's probably in here puking or something! I'll go check!" Erica burst into the bathroom and busted us. "Ooh shit!" She exclaimed loudly.

"What is it?" Darrin came into the bathroom behind Erica, "what the hell is going on?" He yelled.

"Darrin, this isn't what it looks like." Samantha tried to pull her dress down while getting off my lap.

"Really? Cause it looks like you had your tongue down some bitches throat. Is this the same chick that was at your house a couple months ago?"

"I can explain…."

"Yeah, I'm the same chick that was at her house a couple months ago." I stood up.

"Rose, please, let me….."

"Let you what Samantha? For goodness sakes you're wearing my ring while making out with a dyke in the bathroom. Have some fucking class!"

"Dude you not gonna keep calling me out my damn name." I was trying my best to remain calm.

At that moment Jo walked in with two security guards behind her.

"Darrin, I need you to leave the bathroom." She had sobered up a bit.

"I'm not going anywhere until Samantha explains what the fuck is going on."

"Sir, that wasn't a request." One of the guards opened the door and gestured towards the hallway.

He looked around angry but decided getting his ass beat by the two guards wouldn't be in his best interest.

"Everybody good?" Jo asked, looking around and settling her eyes on Erica, who was instantly by her side.

"Perfect timing baby."

"Yeah bro, I'm good. Sam you okay?"

"I don't know. I didn't want this to happen like this." She looked teary eyed around at all of us.

I reached for her hand, "Samantha, I'm sorry I know this doesn't make things easy on you but I meant what I said earlier, I won't wait around on the sidelines while you play house with Darrin. So if you want to be with me like you claim then you'll have to figure it out. If you want to talk you can call me later." I kissed her on the lips and turned to walk out.

"My security will walk you to your car." Jo said as she shook my hand.

"I don't need all that. I told you I'm good."

"Please, it'll make me feel better...." Samantha said quietly.

"Aight." I looked back at Sam before opening the bathroom door. I needed to find Sierra to tell her I was leaving.

As usual, I ran into Charlie first.

"Rose! What's going on? I just saw security escort Darrin out of the club."

"Ummm just a little misunderstanding. I'm sure the twins will fill you in. I'm headed out though. Have you seen Sierra?" I asked after hugging her.

"She was by the bar. Will I see you before I leave?"

"I'm not sure but either way, take care of yourself."

Charlie looked disappointed with my answer but it was time I started making better choices for myself and unfortunately one of those choices might include cutting out Samantha's family.

"Why do I feel like this is goodbye, Rose?"

I just smiled at Charlie and gave her a kiss on the cheek before going to find Sierra.

EPILOGUE

SAMANTHA

———◁✦▷———

I pulled up in front of Darrin's townhouse and took a couple of deep breaths before getting out of the car. It was the morning after the party and now that I had sobered up, I realized just how bad things were between me and…..everyone. Jo thanked me for once again making our birthday about me, surprisingly Charlie hadn't said much. Darrin blew up my phone for hours, I finally called him back when I got home. He didn't believe me when I told him I had misplaced my phone at the club and then it died. He insisted I come to his house last night but I was too drunk to drive so I told him I would come first thing in the morning. He wasn't happy about that so we stayed on FaceTime until I fell asleep. I didn't know exactly what this morning's conversation was going to entail but I wasn't looking forward to it. I let myself in the front door and found Darrin sitting at the dining room table with a mug of coffee.

"Good morning."

"Is it?" He asked, pouring whiskey into the mug.

"It's a little early for you to be drinking, don't you think? It's barely 9 o'clock."

"I haven't stopped drinking since walking in on my fiancé straddling a bitch in the bathroom."

And here we go….

"Darrin, I can explain…"

"How long have you been sleeping with her?"

"I'm not sleeping with her. I haven't even seen Rose in months."

"So you're telling me you've never had sex with her? Cause she seemed real familiar with your body from where I was standing."

I paused for a second debating on how much of the truth I wanted to share. Fuck it, might as well let the cat all the way out of the bag.

"I didn't say I never slept with her. I said I'm not currently sleeping with her."

"Well no shit you're not currently sleeping with her considering you're currently standing here lying to me!" He yelled, causing me to jump.

"Darrin, don't…."

"Don't what?! Don't question you about who you've been fucking? Don't be upset that you've been lying to me for who knows how long? What exactly don't you want me to do Samantha?!"

"Darrin, you're scaring me." I hated that I was crying but I really was scared.

"Good! Maybe if I had scared you before now you wouldn't be whoring around while wearing my damn engagement ring!" He threw his cup across the room and it shattered against the wall.

I turned and practically ran to the front door. I heard him coming behind me and as soon as I opened the door, he reached around me and pushed it shut again.

"I want to leave!"

"Samantha, I'm sorry. I'll calm down."

I didn't move from the door so he added, "I promise I'm calm. I didn't mean to scare you. Please, don't go." He let go of the door and I heard him walk away.

After a few minutes of composing myself and my nerves, I went into the living room and sat on the couch. He was cleaning up the glass and coffee filled whiskey from the wall and floor. When he finished, he handed me a cup of coffee and sat down on the other end of the couch.

"I'm listening," his voice was calm now.

I took a few sips of the coffee and several deep breaths.

"Rose and I met at one of Jo's clubs almost a year ago. We were only friends, she knew all about you and our relationship. She never pressured me into anything more. We slept together once and then I ended the friendship. I didn't want to further jeopardize what we had. I love you and I want to be with you."

"How long ago?"

"Way before you proposed. I hadn't talked to her in months before you proposed and last night was the first time I've seen her since then."

"So you missed her so much that you decided to make out with her in the bathroom?" His voice was still calm but cold, nonetheless.

"No….I had a little too much to drink and…..I…I….don't know." I put my head down and fiddled with my hands and the coffee mug.

"Oh okay, you had too much to drink. That makes it better. I completely understand now. Were you drinking the night you fucked her too?"

I flinched at the question. "I understand you're angry and you have every right to be but if we can't talk about this as civilized people then…..."

"Civilized?" He laughed, "then what? You're going to screw someone else?" He laughed again.

"Darrin….tell me how we can fix this?"

"WE didn't break this…you did. I don't know if this can be fixed. Right now, I'm going to bed. You can let yourself out…" He walked out of the living room and down the hall to the master bedroom.

I sat there silently crying for a few minutes before I got up and left. Once I got home, I decided to see if I could do damage control on the other relationships I had ruined. I tried to call Jo twice but it went straight to voicemail both times so I called Erica.

"Hey girl."

"Hey Sam, how you doing this morning?"

"As well as can be expected. Any chance you're with Jo?" I asked.

"Yeah, she's right here."

"Oh, her phone must be dead. I just tried to call her."

"Baby, Sam just tried to call you," there was silence and then Erica said, "hey she's not up to talking right now. I'll have her call you back in a couple hours."

"Oh….okay. That's cool. You want to hang out later? I could really use the company."

"I'm taking Jo to dinner tonight but we can hang out tomorrow after we get off work."

"Okay. Talk to you guys later."

"Later babes!"

I sighed heavily and hit 'call' on Rose's name before I chickened out.

"Hey Sam." She answered on the second ring.

"Hey….are you busy?"

"I actually just got home from the gym and was about to jump in the shower. Can I call you back once I get out?"

"Okay."

"Okay, call you right back." She hung up. I paced back and forth in my living room waiting for her to call me back and trying to figure out what I was going to say to her when she did. My phone rang and jolted me out of my deep thoughts.

"Hey."

"I'm back. What's up? You okay?"

"Ummm as well as can be expected." I laughed.

"I'm sure. How did everything go after I left last night?"

"Last night wasn't too bad but this morning on the other hand has been a mess. I told Darrin that we slept together."

"Really?"

"Yeah….look Rose I'm sorry about last night and for putting you in the middle of all this. I…"

"Sam, no need to apologize. I played as big a part in what happened last night as you did. However, Sam I meant what I said. As much as I love you, I'm not settling for anything less than whole and since I know that isn't going to happen right now, if ever, I have to say goodbye. I'm not standing on the sidelines being your friend or plaything while you figure out how to truly be happy. I've worked too hard at my own truth and happiness to let anyone jeopardize that. I wish you all the best in whatever you decide to do but I gotta go."

"Rose….I…love you."

"I know and I love you too. When you finally make up your mind and decide you want to be happy then you know how to find me. I can't promise that I'll be waiting but I promise I'll answer if you call. Goodbye Samantha."

"Goodbye Rose."

I threw myself on the couch like a two-year-old having a temper tantrum and bawled my eyes out. What the fuck is wrong with me? Did I really just lose Darrin and Rose on the same day? The bigger question was why did Rose saying goodbye hurt 1,000 times more than when Darrin said it? I knew the answer but was I finally ready to admit it to myself? To the world?

JOSEPHINE

"Jo, I don't like being in the middle of you and Samantha."

"I'm not asking you to be in the middle of anything. She called your phone looking for me, not the other way around." I answered nonchalantly while flipping through the channels.

"I know she did. Did you block her? Because your phone is definitely not dead."

"Soooo do you want to be left out of it or not?" I could see her giving me the evil eye out of the corner of my eye but I didn't turn to face her.

"I know you can see my face but you're right so fine don't answer the question. Just so we're clear on where I stand, I don't like this one bit and I'm not going to be passing messages or playing mediator between you two. Okay?"

"Yep, I'm clear babe. Have you seen this movie? I heard it was really good." I knew how Erica felt when Sam and I fought so it was pointless to even get into it with her. Plus I didn't want her to feel like she had to choose sides so instead I'll just avoid the conversation all together. "I'm going to make some popcorn. Need anything?" I kissed her before going into the kitchen.

"A bottle of tequila."

"Hey, thanks for meeting me." I hugged Rose when she showed up to the restaurant.

"No problem. Everything okay?"

"Shit I should be asking you that. How are you?"

"I don't even know. I'm pissed that I even allowed myself to get caught up in this shit again. I'm pissed that I'm still in love with your sister. I'm pissed that she's still in love with me but insists on being with someone else. I guess overall I'm just pissed."

"So she told you that she was still going to be with Darrin?"

"She didn't have to. She's too chicken to live her truth. What am I supposed to do with that? If she's not bold enough to love herself then I can't expect her to love me."

"Yeah you're right about that. Sam has always been so confident and sure of herself. I don't know why she's struggling with this so much. Anyway, I just wanted to check on you and see how you were doing. I was kind of hoping things would work out between you two."

"Shit me too!" She laughed. "Look, whatever happens or doesn't happen between me and Samantha, I hope that we can still be friends."

"No doubt. Besides, I'm still praying that somehow you guys will find your way back to each other. You belong together."

"Keep those prayers coming man. Maybe between the two of us, God will answer them."

"Amen to that."

DARRIN

I slept until about ten o'clock at night after Samantha left. Half of me hoped that she would have put up more of a fight about leaving but it was for the best. I was so angry knowing that she had cheated on me….and with a woman. My mind was spinning with questions, revelations and accusations. I wanted to call her but I needed to get a hold of my emotions first and figure out if I even wanted this relationship. I loved Samantha and thought we were going to spend the rest of our lives together but that was before I found out she was gay….well whatever the hell she is. I needed to talk to someone but Robert would say I told you so and I damn sure couldn't tell my mom, she loved Samantha as much as I did. I didn't want to break her heart the way mine was. Guess I was all alone in this. Well there was one person I could call…..

"Hey. You up? I need to talk about Samantha. No, I'll come to you after I shower. Okay."

About an hour later I rang the doorbell and Bianca opened the door. She was wearing cute pajamas and her hair was in a bun.

"What happened?" She asked as we walked into the kitchen and sat at the island.

"She cheated on me…..with a woman." I added.

"Wow! She was right! How did you find out?"

"Who was right?"

"Me and Kelly ran into her having lunch with some butch looking broad like a year ago. It looked kind of suspect but I didn't think Ms. Perfect would do something like that."

"And you didn't think to tell me that? I walked in on her and the butch looking broad making out in the bathroom at her party last night."

"Double wow! It wasn't my place to tell you anything. You broke it off with me, remember? So now what? Are you guys done?"

"I don't know. She said she wants to be with me but we haven't really had a conversation yet."

"Well….what do you want?"

"I have no fucking clue."

"What about counseling? Do you think it will help?"

"Maybe. I guess it's worth a shot to see if the relationship can be salvaged."

"You know you love her so I say why not." She shrugged her shoulders. "I told you, you should have given that ring to me anyway." She smirked.

"I should have. If counseling doesn't work then uh…." I offered.

"If you want me to hold on to that possibility then you gotta give me something to look forward to. The way you look in those gray sweatpants, it's a strong possibility." Janelle licked her lips.

"I think that can be arranged." I loosened the drawstring on my sweatpants and she slid off her stool and onto her knees in front of me.

The next morning, on my way to work, I called Samantha. I had decided what I wanted.

"Hello?" She sounded like she was still asleep.

"Are you not going to work today?" I asked in lieu of a greeting.

"No, I have a migraine so I'm going to work from home."

"Okay. So what is it that you want Samantha?" I got straight to the point.

"I want to make this work." She answered.

"Good, I want that too. So we're going to go to counseling."

"We can do that. Do you have someone in mind?"

"I don't. I also want to move."

"I'll look for someone today. Like move in together? I don't know about that…."

"Yes, move in together….in Spain."

"In Spain?!"

"Yes I was offered a position there and I turned it down but now I think it's a good idea for us."

"Darrin….Spain? My family...my career…"

"Those are my stipulations if you want this to work. The move won't be for another 7-8 months so that gives you time to think about it and for us to be in counseling."

"Okay."

"Okay, you'll go?"

"Okay I'll go to counseling with you and think about the move."

"I'll take that for now. I'll pick you up when I get off work and we can go to dinner. It would be great if you could have an appointment set up by then."

"I'll try."

"Okay," I disconnected the call.

ERICA

"Hey bestie. Do you want coffee? I'm going to stop by Dunkin on my way to the office?"

"No thanks. I'm actually going to work from home today. I woke up with a migraine. Well I actually went to sleep with a migraine."

"Aww sorry boo. You still want me to come by after work?"

"Yeah if you want. Ooh why don't you come work from my house too?"

"Cause I actually have some work to do." I laughed.

"You do know I own the company, right?"

"Yes, I am aware. And even though I enjoy the perks of being your best friend. I don't want to take advantage of it."

"Ugh, why do you have to be such a good employee."

I laughed, "I tell you what. If I can get the important stuff done then I'll bring lunch and spend the rest of the day with you. Cool?"

"That sounds like a plan. I'll see you later."

"See you later!"

"Thanks for lunch Erica."

"No problem. So you've been really quiet since I got here. What's been going on since the other night?" I leaned back in the chair and pulled my feet up under me.

"Everything. Rose told me she is done and if I decide that I want to be with her, then call her, however she's not waiting for me."

"Damn."

"And I don't know what to say about Darrin. I thought he was going to hit me."

"What?!"

"He didn't hit me but I was really scared. He called me this morning and said that we're going to counseling and that he wants us to move to Spain."

"Girl hell no? So how bad did he flip out when you told him no?"

"I told him I would go to counseling and I would think about Spain. I have about 7 to 8 months to decide."

"What's there to think about? Are you seriously thinking about moving to Spain with him? Especially after you just said you thought he was going to hit you."

"I don't know. I just need to do what I can to get him to trust me again."

"Samantha I love you and I have to be honest and tell you I think you are making a big mistake. You are in love with Rose. The sooner you stop running from that reality the sooner you can be happy and you all can start to move on from everything that has happened. First, you need to accept that she is the one and not Darrin. You're just prolonging the inevitable and you're going to end up losing her for real."

"I gotta take this call. If I don't answer when he FaceTimes me he'll get upset." Sam got up from the couch and walked into the kitchen to answer her phone.

Aww hell, this girl done lost her damn mind.

"Erica, why can't we just enjoy dinner without going back to the same conversation?" Jo sighed and put her fork down.

"Because it's been three weeks, Jo. I mean come on and just talk to her already."

"I hope you were this persistent with her when she didn't talk to me for several months."

"I was. I told her she was being stubborn and stupid just like you are being now."

"Well I appreciate you speaking up then and now but I really don't want to have this conversation again….not tonight."

I opened and shut my mouth a couple of times while I debated if this was worth us getting into a fight over. I finally decided it wasn't and picked up my glass of water instead.

"How was work?" I finally asked.

"It was really good. I'm glad it's Friday though." Jo smiled.

"Me too. It's been a long week with you having to go in early and us not sleeping together. I think I actually missed you."

"You think? Girl, stop playing, you know you missed me and all my many attributes." She rolled her tongue at me.

I rolled my eyes, "anyway. You still want to try the new hookah spot I told you about?"

"Yeah we can go when we leave here." Jo signaled to the waitress for the check.

An hour later we were settled in a corner booth with drinks and a hookah. The vibe and music in the lounge was nice. I could feel Jo staring at me as I swayed to the music.

"What?" I asked.

"Nothing, just admiring my woman, that's all."

"Well cut it out. You're making me nervous." I stared off towards the bar, "damn she's sexy."

Jo cocked her head to the side and followed my gaze. There was a pretty, Hispanic looking chick at the bar. She had on a tight dress, high heels and her long hair was flowing freely down her back.

"Damn if you gonna stare like that, you might as well invite her over. Hell, why don't you take her home?" Jo said with a smirk.

"Okay." I threw back the rest of my drink, licked my lips, pushed up my tits and got up.

"Okay what? Where are you going?"

I was already halfway across the floor. I walked up to the chick, rested my hand on the small of her back and whispered in her ear, "my girlfriend just dared me to come ask you to sit with us. We both think you are sexy as hell."

She laughed and then we both looked over towards Jo. "I'm Erica. How about you?"

"I'm Reina. It's nice to meet you, Erica."

"The pleasure is mine. Reina, I get the feeling you're a….free spirit. Am I right?" I asked seductively.

"Yeah, you're right. Are you going to take me to meet your girlfriend?"

I grabbed her hand and headed back to our booth.

"Baby this is Reina. Reina, this is Jo."

"Nice to meet you, Jo." She sat down next to Jo.

"Nice to meet you too, Reina." Jo answered. I knew she was wondering what I was up to as I sat down on the other side of Reina.

"How long have you two been together?"

"Almost a year. Well if you count the time we were dating." Jo answered.

"Nice. I was with my last girlfriend for three years."

"What happened?" I asked.

"She wanted to move out of state but I had just gotten a promotion at work so I wasn't feeling it. We tried to do long distance for a while but it just didn't work. We're still friends....with benefits." Reina laughed.

"Ooh I like those kinds of friends." I rubbed one of Reina's legs while watching Jo to gauge her reaction. She sat back and pulled on the hookah.

Oh so she wants a show, I thought to myself.

"Reina, can I kiss you?"

"As long as your girl is okay with it."

I looked over at Jo again, she nodded. I turned Reina's face towards mine and licked my lips before kissing her. One of us moaned but I'm not sure who it was. I could feel myself getting wetter by the millisecond. Her lips were so soft and she was a really good kisser. After a few minutes, Jo cleared her throat. Reina pulled back first and wiped her lips, giggling.

"Mmmm do you guys want to get out of here? I don't live far."

"How about you give me your number and we take a rain check? Jo has to get up early for work and I wouldn't want to rush the fun." I rubbed the back of my hand up and down Reina's arm.

"Aww okay." Reina pouted as she put her number in my phone. "I hope you'll call me soon."

"Goodnight Reina." Jo finally spoke up while watching my heavy breathing.

She stood up and kissed me again on the lips before turning towards Jo and blowing her a kiss.

"Can you make it to the house?" She asked after Reina was gone.

I shook my head no.

"Me either, bathroom or car?"

"Car." We stood up and Jo dropped three fifty-dollar bills on the table which more than covered our check and tip.

I grabbed my purse and we walked outside to the valet stand. While waiting for someone to bring Jo's truck around, I leaned over and whispered in Jo's ear, "did you bring the strap?"

She nodded yes and smiled. I hopped in the driver's seat of her truck when the valet arrived. Jo got in the backseat which I'm sure looked strange. We rode in silence and by the time I pulled into the parking lot of an office complex, Jo already had the strap on and was ready to go. I climbed over the seat and onto Jo's lap.

"Why am I not surprised that you're not wearing panties.?" Jo asked and flicked her thumb over my clit but I moved her hand and slid the thick rubber dick inside of me. I sat there a minute, panting, waiting for my body to adjust to the girth. After a few seconds, I reached down to the remote laying on the seat and turned on the vibration that was for Jo's pleasure.

"Shit!" She exclaimed when she felt that it was on full speed. "Someone's in a rush."

It wasn't long before I was riding her fast and hard. Jo thrust upwards to meet me and it was my turn to yell, "shit! Fuck, I'm about to cum already." Jo grabbed my hips and held me in place while she continued to thrust upwards into me and grind her hips slowly in between thrusts. The mix of both was driving me crazy. My body did it's usual little convulsion indicating I was cumming. After a few more minutes of the slow grinds Jo's release finally came. She switched the vibration off and we both sat there trying to catch our breath.

"Damn woman. Care to explain?"

"If you need me to explain that then clearly we aren't doing it right?" I joked as I climbed off her lap and sat on the seat next to her.

"Don't be a smart ass. You know what I mean."

"Reina? I just thought I would kick it up a notch." I shrugged nonchalantly.

"Mmhmm and just how far were you willing to kick it up?"

"How far would you let me?"

"Far enough to get to this point."

"Is that it? Nothing more?"

"What exactly are you asking E?"

"I don't know. What are your thoughts on threesomes?"

"I've never thought much about them. I mean I've had them but never with someone I'm serious with so I don't know."

"So if I said I wanted to give it a try…..?"

"I'd say let me think about it and get back to you."

"That's fair. You ready to go?"

"Again? Damn girl you trying to kill me!"

"I meant go home, crazy!" I laughed.

"Oh….yeah. Let's go." Jo pulled her pants up, leaving the strap on.

"Although, when we get to whoever's home we're going to, I might need to go again."

"Of course you do." Jo playfully rolled her eyes at me and got out of the car so she could drive us to her home, since it was closer.

ROSE

"Hello."

"So you are alive."

"I text you…."

"You text me that you weren't feeling well and you were leaving the club. You haven't responded to a text or a phone call since then. You made it clear that we aren't dating but damn I at least thought we were friends." Sierra sounded pissed.

"You're right and I really am sorry. The truth is I thought I was ready to see my ex but I wasn't. And especially not with her new fiance. It was not my intention to dip out on you like that but I really needed to get out of there before I did something I would regret."

"So now you're just going to sit around in a funk because she wasn't smart enough to see that you're a catch?"

"What makes you think I'm a catch? I could be an asshole."

"Based on your recent behaviors that sounds very accurate."

"Ouch, I deserve that."

"You do." She laughed, "look Rose, I get it and I've been there. I know it's not easy to get back out there and start dating again. Maybe it's too soon or maybe the time is just right. You know they say the best way to get over someone is to get under someone else."

"Is that what they say?" It was my time to laugh a little.

"Yep! But all jokes aside if you ever need a friend, I'm here. And when you're ready for more than a friend, I might still be here for that too."

"Wait, why is it a might? A minute ago I was a catch?" I asked playfully and realized I was flirting.

"A minute ago, you were also an asshole. Let's not get cocky."

"Oh you got jokes. What are you doing later? You want to hang out? As friends?"

"Let me check my calendar and get back to you?"

"Okay well you do that and let me know."

"Looks like I might be free."

"What time should I pick you up?"

"Uh uh this isn't a date. I'll drive and pay for myself. I don't want you getting confused and falling for me."

"You're on a real roll today. How about we meet at Atlantic Station at 6?"

"That works. Later!"

"Thanks Sierra."

"Anytime friend."

Other Books in the Series

The Other Side: The Reveal

Sam has finally found herself or so she thinks. She knows who she wants to be with, but will it be too late for their future? Will Samantha's journey to the other side all be for nothing? Will Jo and Erica's quest for spice and adventure jeopardize everything they're building? Will a heavy case from Rose's past destroy lifelong friendships? Will Charlie finally put herself and her family before the needs of her sisters? Find out all this and more in The Reveal!

Subscribe for updates and other exclusive content at:
www.authorojaybarr.com

www.ingramcontent.com/pod-product-compliance
Lightning Source LLC
Chambersburg PA
CBHW031314271224
19565CB00014B/938